ENOUGH ABOUT LOVE

Enough About Love

HERVÉ LE TELLIER

· · ·

TRANSLATED FROM THE FRENCH BY ADRIANA HUNTER

OTHER PRESS
NEW YORK

Originally published in French as *Assez parlé d'amour* by Éditions
Jean-Claude Lattès, Paris 2009.
Translation Copyright © 2010 Adriana Hunter

Production Editor: *Yvonne E. Cárdenas*
Book design: *Simon M. Sullivan*
This book was set in 11.75 pt Adobe Garamond
by Alpha Design & Composition of Pittsfield, NH.
Stag beetle illustration on page 255 copied from Albrecht Dürer
by Marie Berville

10 9 8 7 6 5 4 3 2 1

LIBRARY OF CONGRESS CATALOGING-IN-PUBLICATION DATA

Le Tellier, Hervé, 1957-
[Assez parlé d'amour. English]
Enough about love / by Hervé Le Tellier ; translated from the French by
Adriana Hunter.
p. cm.
Originally published in French as Assez parlé d'amour.
ISBN 978-1-59051-399-6 (trade pbk.) — ISBN 978-1-59051-400-9
(ebk.) 1. Married people—Fiction. 2. Middle-aged persons—Fiction.
3. Adultery—Fiction. I. Hunter, Adriana. II. Title.
PQ2672.E11455A9213 2011
843'.914—dc22
2010040656

FOR SARAH

For me, love has always been
the most important of matters, or rather the only one.

STENDHAL, *The Life of Henry Brulard*

PROLOGUE

. . .

THAT YEAR THE PLANET EXPERIENCED its hottest autumn for five centuries. But the climate's providential clemency, which may have played its part, will not be mentioned again.

This tale covers a period of three months, and perhaps a little more. Any man—or woman—who wants to hear nothing—or no more—about love should put this book down.

THOMAS

. . .

OWNS SHOULD BE GIVEN LARGE PARKS. Parks are a condition necessary for young people's lives to change course, to set off on a different tack, down an unforeseen fork. For them to realize part of their potential. It is into just such a park, the Jardin du Luxembourg in Paris, that a young man walks one February morning in 1974. He has long hair and is wearing a woolen scarf, his name is Thomas, Thomas Le Gall.

Thomas is a good student. He is just sixteen and is already in his first year of an advanced math class: he has to satisfy his mother's ambitions for him, and get into one of the elite universities, ideally the highly competitive Polytechnique. But on this February morning, Thomas left home—he lives in Barbès in the Eighteenth Arrondissement—and took the Métro, and did not get off at the station where his school is. He stayed on Line 4 all the way to Saint-Michel, then walked up the boulevard to the park. He walks toward the large pond, passes statues

of the queens of France, and sits on a metal chair. He has prepared for this getaway: he has several books in his bag. It is not
all that cold.

In the evening he goes home to his parents. He is hungry: he
had a baguette sandwich and a piece of fruit for lunch.

The next day, the day after that, and every other day,
Thomas goes back to the Jardin du Luxembourg. The park
becomes his headquarters. He sometimes meets up with bohemian companions: a girl his age, Manon, blond, ski-jump nose
and freckles, even more adrift than he is (the smell of patchouli
will remind him of her forever); and Kader, a tall black man,
maybe thirty, a guitarist who plays in the Métro. When it rains,
Thomas takes shelter by one of the kiosks or warms up at the
Malebranche, a smoky café where he quickly falls into a routine with some art students from Louis-le-Grand. They discuss
politics and literature, row about Proust, Althusser, Trotsky,
and Barthes, his vehemence in proportion to his ignorance of
the texts. When he comes to read them properly, later, he will
blush as he remembers the idiocies he uttered, and marvel at
the impunity of his imposture.

March comes, then April. Thomas has informed the teach-
ers that he has abandoned his studies. To his parents, of course,
he lies. He discovers how easy that is, exciting even, how gifted
he is at lying. He reeks of tobacco? He rants about how stressed
smokers get before their practice exams. He is short of money
at lunchtime? From now on the cafeteria likes you to pay with
cash, he says he suspects the bursar of corruption. He comes
home too early by mistake? An oxidation-reduction experiment
went wrong and the chemistry teacher—"You're not going to
believe this"—burned himself. He never talked about his studies so much until the day he quit them.

One May evening, almost before he has set foot in the house, Thomas starts elaborating that day's fiction. His father watches him, in silence. All at once his mother explodes. They know. The school called: he failed to return a book to the library, even though he defected three months ago. Angry words, flaring tempers, big arguments. Thomas will never be admitted to one of the elite universities. He leaves his family home and finds refuge at a friend's house. He lives off small jobs—still possible in those days of a healthy economy—and vaguely takes up studying psychology and sociology, prolonging his adolescence by ten years. One May morning, a telephone call from a police station ejects him brutally from this cocoon. The woman he loves, Piette, who had been hospitalized for depression, has only just been released. She has thrown herself under a train. In three days Thomas completes all the paperwork, organizes the ceremony and buries his friend. With the grave filled, he goes home. He does not emerge until a week later, clean-shaven and with his curly black hair as good as shaved off. He goes back to his studies.

At the point where this story begins, a copper sign screwed to the door frame of 28 rue Monge, not that far from the Jardin du Luxembourg, summarizes his trajectory.

DR. THOMAS LE GALL

PSYCHIATRIST, PSYCHOANALYST

FORMER INTERN AT THE

PARIS PSYCHIATRIC HOSPITALS

The sign paints a professional portrait of him, but when all is said and done, Thomas Le Gall is very professional now.

On the fourth floor, through the door on the left, a one-bedroom apartment has become a psychoanalyst's office. Thomas has kept the spacious modern kitchen. He occasionally eats there, perhaps a spring roll from the Chinese restaurant. The bedroom, to the left of the front door, is now a waiting room: waxed floorboards, two deep armchairs, and a coffee table give it an English country club feel; the window has no curtains and looks out onto the street. The thirty-minute sessions are held at hourly intervals, patients never meet. On set days Thomas sees patients in the large living room: the view of the sky and the plane trees in the courtyard would be clear, if not for exotic wood blinds filtering the light. The door is padded with black velvet. The olive-colored leather of the couch is intended to be soothing. African masks watch over the room benevolently, like the Moai statues, turning their backs to the sea and protecting Easter Island. Behind the Louis-Philippe desk hangs a blue-gray industrial landscape by Lowry. On the opposite wall there is a very small and very dark painting by Bram Van Velde, dating from his friendship with Matisse. It is the only valuable piece. Thomas acquired it at the Drouot auction house, probably paying a little too much—if it actually makes sense to talk about paying too much for art—with the precise intention of stopping himself from buying things at Drouot.

Thomas is well aware that he has made this space a caricature of a psychoanalyst's office. At least he has spared his patients the Malian sculptures and Congolese nail fetishes. But decorum and what it represents are not without importance, and Thomas knows this.

On the extensive bookshelves against the far wall, literature rubs shoulders with psychoanalysis in peaceful conflict. Joyce mingles with Pierre Kahn, Leiris is shoehorned against Lacan, a book by Queneau which has been put back in the wrong place—a good sign for a book—leans up against a Deleuze.

When Queneau died, Thomas was not yet fifteen. *Si tu crois xava, xava xava xa, xava durer toujours la saison des za la saison des zamours* . . .[1] It is a long time since Thomas Le Gall has believed it will. The wrinkles are growing deeper, his curly hair, now more salt than pepper, is receding from his forehead, the face has broadened, is thickening slightly, the former forty-year-old is heading toward the sixty-year-old and is expecting worse to come.

The bow-fronted clock on the mantelpiece says nine o'clock. Thomas has deactivated its chiming mechanism to keep control of his sessions. He sits in his armchair, waiting. He reads a two-day-old copy of *Le Monde*, tidies a few papers. His first appointment is late. Anna Stein is always late. By two, ten, sometimes fifteen minutes, always for a good reason: the babysitter didn't arrive, Paris traffic jams, nowhere to park. Thomas suggested a different time to her, she turned it down. Perhaps she likes playing hard to get. Thomas trusts the wisdom of popular expressions.

Anna Stein. Twelve years of treatment, now reaching the end. For the first few years, like many people, Anna did nothing but talk. She unrolled her life. Then when she had exhausted her recollections, grappled every crumb of memory, she felt like a river that had run dry, been spent, used up, and she could not think straight for a year, perhaps more. It was when she admitted defeat, when she gave up, angrily—"Well, what else do you want me to say?"—that she could start talking without thinking, to say, as Freud put it, "whatever came into her head," without trying to re-create some fiction or construct a logical

1. If you think it'll, itll itll itll, go on forever, this season of, unov unov, season of love . . .

narrative. Now Anna makes associations, discovers links, reestablishes meaning. She is getting somewhere.

Two days earlier, in the last minute of the session, she blurted: "I've met someone. I've met with someone. A man, a writer." In the big book dedicated to Anna Stein, Thomas merely jotted down a few words, unhurriedly, "met with someone"—the pleonasm intrigued him—then added "man," "writer." On the left, he isolates what he perceives to be factual about something, on the right he underlines what he feels is caught in the words, sifting out the formalities. Anna added, "a real thunderbolt." Thomas was amused by the expression, so electric and unequivocal.

Then, in pencil, he drew a dotted line, and at the end of it he wrote the letter X, which he linked to the A of Anna. Changing perspective, shifting logic, he associated the two letters X and A in an oval diagram, a Boolean notation. He did not press her for more information. His Westminster clock was already several minutes past the half hour. He simply said: "See you on Thursday."

ANNA

. . .

ANNA STEIN IS ABOUT TO TURN FORTY. She looks ten
years younger in these well-heeled circles where the
norm is more like five. But the imminence of this expiration
date and the witchery of the number itself send a chill through
her, and to think she still feels she is in the comet's tail of her
teens. Forty . . . Because she thinks there is a *before* and an
after, as in commercials for hair products, she is already living
in mourning for what has been and in terror of what is yet to
come.

Childhood memory: Anna is seven, one sister, two brothers, the youngest barely talking yet, she is the eldest. It is not
easy being the big one, the one who is argued with because the
others are too little. But Anna the charmer managed to remain
her mother's favorite. She sits her brothers and her sister around
her in a semicircle. The golden light pouring through the window is that of a day coming to a close, probably a Sunday spent

in the country. She is standing, book in hand, reading out loud. She spices up the story, which is too straightforward for her liking, with dragons and fairies, ogres and princes, and it all becomes very muddled, she even gets lost herself in places. The children listen to their happy, glowing big sister, fascinated, captivated, frightened too. Gesticulating wildly with her arms, sometimes jumping about, Anna mimes the action and makes sure her intonation sustains the attention of her young audience. She has no doubt: she will be an actress, or a dancer, or a singer.

At fifteen, Anna ties her black hair up to reveal the nape of her neck. She triumphantly inhabits her brand-new woman's body: she wears leopard-skin leggings and high heels, aggressive bras. She dreams of a life in the public eye, a career under the spotlight, and the names of cities—New York, Buenos Aires, Shanghai—make her swoon. She starts a rock band with herself as the singer, and baptizes them Anna and Her Three Lovers. The lead guitarist, bass player, and drummer are all in love with her, after all. In vain in all three cases, one a little less than the others, but so little.

At twenty, Anna looks elegant in her medical student's white overalls. She chose one that barely fit her, sacrificing comfort for elegance, wearing it open one button too low at the front, and, as her shoes are the only other thing that show, she puts a great deal of energy into picking them out. Often they are fluorescent. Over the years she becomes Dr. Stein. Intelligent but with a dilettante attitude, she passes every exam: she is probably too proud to mess up in her studies. She is not yet proud enough to dare to *want* to fail. The adventurous life that would have required so many transgressions is now further and further from her, and she knows that, despite her long legs and beautiful breasts, she will never dance in cabarets. Her mother is a doctor and Anna becomes a psychiatrist, she marries a surgeon, also Jewish, they have two children, Karl, then Lea. "A little Jewish business," she sometimes laughs. But she has kept something from when she was twenty, a hint of nostalgia for the bohemian: a bold quality in her walk, a light in her smile. Her own tactful way of admitting that she has never completely given up the idea of the stage.

Yes, Anna became Dr. Stein. But does she completely believe it?

Once when she called the hospital to speak to a colleague, she said confidently: "Hello, could I speak to Dr. Stein please?"

Utterly stunned, she hung up immediately, praying the receptionist had not recognized her voice. It was more than an hour before she had the courage to call back.

THOMAS AND LOUISE

· · ·

"THUNDERBOLT." At first Thomas Le Gall smiled to hear Anna use that expression. He did not ask whether she had counted the seconds between the flash of lightning and the sound of thunder. But life is facetious: a few hours after that appointment with Anna, Thomas was to be struck by a thunderbolt too. It would be at the "ritual" dinner held by Sammy Karamanlis, a young sociologist who held an open house evening once a month. Thomas did not know Sammy, but a friend took him along: "You won't be bored, you'll meet people, pretty women, delightful people."

Sammy lives in a one-bedroom apartment on the rue de Grenelle, just where the Seventh Arrondissement likes to think it is already part of the Latin Quarter: high ceilings, bourgeois furnishings, views onto a massive paved courtyard. It would be improbably luxurious for an employee of the National Center for Scientific Research if the researcher's father were not involved in banking in Lausanne. The guests, about thirty of them, seem to be regulars, but their conversations only rarely roam in the direction of their private lives. Thomas circulates discreetly from one group to another: someone else might have fun diagnosing a case of hysteria here, a breakdown pending there, the odd depression. Thomas knows how social posturing can mislead with its pretenses, appearances, and control. He forbids himself opinions.

He quickly notices a young woman with short blond hair, pale eyes, and a lot of people around her. She is leaning against the wall in the huge hallway, holding an orange-colored cocktail glass, its surface quivering from her voluble conversation. Thomas moves closer, listens. He grasps that she is a lawyer. She is talking about Chinese, Albanian, and Romanian mafias, about their extreme violence, their explicit threats, about the interpreters who dare not translate every word, she describes terrified witnesses and the sinking fear in her stomach when she looks into the cold eyes of a killer. Three weeks earlier, a Romanian pimp bound one of his girls' hands and feet, gagged her with duct tape, and threw her in the bathtub. Then, slowly, with a razor, he slashed her, really deeply, almost cutting her into pieces. All the blood drained out of her, "two or three hours," the pathologist reckoned. So that they knew what he was capable of, he made all his girls file through the bathroom, one after another, forcing them to touch the blood-soaked woman who was still gasping for breath, her eyes bulging with fear and pain. She eventually died. A colleague has to defend this man, and the young lawyer is haunted by the case. Just by describing it again, she relives the nightmare that words still cannot drive away.

With a pretty flick of her hand she pushes back a drooping lock of hair, she suddenly notices him and smiles: Thomas knows instantly that he is caught, and is happy to be. He feels an irresistible magnetic draw, one he takes pleasure in resisting. A pull that would be called attraction in physics too. He gathers the woman's name is Louise, then she specifies: Louise Blum. She has fine features and is slim enough to emphasize her muscularity. What else to say about her, how to discern what he finds so erotic? The fleeting certainty, he will think later, that she smiled only at him? And he repeats it to himself: Louise Blum. He thinks how totally she suits her name.

As luck would have it, they end up sitting next to each other, but who believes in luck? She is still talking about organized crime and the role of defense lawyers, because there must be a defense, after all. He stays rather quiet, because he does not want to fill any gaps with his own words and also because he prefers listening to her. He likes her voice, the immediacy she injects into verbs. Then, when she shows an interest in him, he thinks he is telling her what he does but only says the word "analyst." "Analyst?" she repeats, as if suspecting him of being an economist or a financier. He adds the *psycho-*. She behaves as if she is fascinated, perhaps she really is? Though she acts all anxious: "I often do slightly weird things. Like I talk to myself. Do you think I should have analysis?"

"Everyone should have analysis. It should be compulsory, like military service used to be."

Thomas is only half joking. She nods.

"I know a place where everyone does, a whole nation of analyzed people: the East Village in New York. Never seen so many crazy people per square foot."

Her laugh is deep in her throat, slightly hoarse, a laugh he instantly loves.

They play a social game: they look for things they have in common. And have no trouble finding some. He knows a psychiatrist friend of hers by reputation, she knows a lawyer he has done business with.

"He's a complete asshole!" she says without a moment's hesitation. It was not a slipup because she laughs as she adds, "He's not a close friend of yours, is he?"

Thomas shakes his head, flustered, but then nods: true, he is a complete asshole. By digging deeper, they also find some journalists, a few artists . . .

"Pathetic," smiles Louise.

"What?"

"How small the world is . . . No one ever just falls out of the sky."

"I'm so sorry," sighs Thomas.

His answer is formulaic but sorry he is, all the same. He would like to have fallen out of the sky. But they have found common ground, there is a familiarity between them—with her leading the way—that feels natural.

Very early on, in passing, she refers to a husband, children. From the twinge of disappointment these words produce, Thomas realizes how attracted he is to Louise. But he cannot draw any conclusions from the way she says them, certainly not that Louise is trying to convince him, or herself, that their meeting has no right to lead to anything. No, for the whole dinner, he leaves his experience as an analyst at the door. It is also true that, sometimes, women who say they have a husband and two children are just saying they have a husband and two children. Hey, he thinks at one point, Louise Blum could be Anna Stein's blond twin. They are alike, they really are, even their lives are similar.

It is getting late, the evening is coming to an end, Louise hands out her e-mail address and telephone number. She has run out of business cards so she scribbles her details on the ends of napkins, which she tears off carefully. He folds the piece she hands to him and puts it in his pocket; on the way home he will check—twice—that he has not lost it, and as soon as he is home he will put the information on his computer and in his cell phone.

On this late summer's morning, as he waits for Anna Stein, Thomas is writing this first e-mail to Louise Blum, so belatedly—he made a point of waiting a whole day—and so careful with respect to what he truly wants: "Thank you for such a nice evening, even though I wasn't in great form. I hope I'll see you again soon, at Sammy's or somewhere else. Thomas (the analyst) XOXO." Well, it's hardly original, Thomas thinks. But if Louise replies despite his banal e-mail, that would at least prove she has some interest in him. He stretches in his chair, reaching his arms up and yawning loudly, a common gesture for the body to dispel the mind's agitation. Click. Send. His Mac imitates a gust of wind and his nine o'clock appointment rings the buzzer. Anna Stein is ten minutes late.

ANNA AND YVES

. . .

ANNA STEIN'S OUTFIT IS DISTINCTIVE, as usual. Wide white pants that fit tightly over her buttocks to define them clearly, a fleetingly transparent, midnight blue blouse, and a shiny, black trench coat. She chooses her clothes carefully, her long tall figure allowing her to wear things that would be fatal on others. She sees herself as slim, lives being slim as synonymous with being rigorous. Gaining weight, she is convinced, is always a lapse.

Anna Stein sits down and apologizes for being late: her little girl, Lea, has a fever *and* there was nowhere to park. She gets comfortable on the couch and goes straight back to the meeting she mentioned the day before yesterday. She repeats the words she used then—he is a writer—and reveals his name, Yves. Thomas erases the X in his diagram from before, replaces it with a Y, and draws a second oval around the A to include her and her husband, Stanislas. Finally, he draws a third one, still including Anna Stein, but to which he adds his own name,

Thomas. Anna Stein is now at the intersection of three rings, and no longer seems to belong to any of them.

Yves is "the same age as Stan," her husband, "or not much older." She thinks he is "pretty broke" and "besides, he lives in Belleville." Writing has always been a fantasy for Anna Stein; she suspects Yves may be its embodiment. She has had no appetite for a week. "I don't eat anything anymore, I've already lost five pounds, at least." It seems to frighten her. "I don't know what's happening to me." The evening of the very day they met, almost before she got through the door at home, she thinks she admitted everything to Stan. All she said, speaking casually as if discussing some pleasant surprise, was that she had met a man at a reception, "a man she found unsettling," "for the first time in a long time." Stan could find nothing to say in response and almost immediately talked about something else, Lea's music theory lesson, how well she was getting on, an appointment Anna's brother had made for a vision problem. Anna Stein would have liked her husband to react or, better, for him to act, for him to know instinctively that she was only saying it so he would hold her back. But Stanislas did not grasp, or did not want to grasp, the weight of her words. He allowed a window to be opened to her desires, and it makes her furious, disappointed, and delighted all at once.

Yves gave her his latest book, with the unusual title *The Two-Leaf Clover*, and wrote the most anodyne of dedications in it. The book, which is very short, relates with ferocious intensity an emotional disaster, a restrained and clinical dissection of a lover's fantasy: a story as old as time itself about an older man who, having become infatuated with a young woman and having seduced her a bit, but not enough, decides to go and join her in Ireland—which explains the title—where he collides head-on with her withering indifference in the most magnificent fiasco. The irony with which it is told made her laugh, and she thought: this man's an expert. She also found it reassuring that she liked his style, his lightness of touch. She is an attentive reader, critical and perceptive, she would have hated him to disappoint her, for him to write like someone who churned out novels, but she was probably in no state to be disappointed. She liked the fact that he could talk about love like that. But something in the way she says "talk about love" this morning makes it sound like an actual character. Thomas writes a note.

Because Thomas is paying close attention, meticulous attention even, it is one of those morning sessions when he will hardly say anything, when he will only ask Anna Stein to repeat a few sentences so that she realizes later that those were the exact sentences she spoke. He jots them down, classifies them, organizes them. If she were to forget them, he would make a point of sending them back to her, like a good baseline player on the tennis court. Years of experience have convinced him of the key role language plays, but he is wary of interpreting things too literally.

Thomas is interested in Yves: surely he himself is this older man who becomes infatuated with a younger woman? Maybe he will read one of his books, why not the very one that seduced Anna Stein? An attentive reader will always learn more, and more quickly, from good authors than from life. Perhaps because there is a strong analogy between psychoanalysis and writing. Like the analyst, the writer wants to be heard, recognized, and is afraid of being swallowed up in thought and words. Most likely Thomas also sees Yves as his own double. Perhaps Anna Stein is aware of this possible reading, of this turning point in her analysis. He is suddenly worried that his own situation might insinuate itself between them. In all the momentum drawing him toward Louise Blum, Anna Stein's words have particular resonance. He must be sure to keep his distance.

THOMAS AND LOUISE

• • •

THE SESSION ENDS when the screen of his Mac flashes discreetly. The name and surname appear in dark blue: Louise Blum. She has replied, already. Thomas feels his breathing quicken, finds this irritating. He sees Anna to the door, says goodbye with measured poise, better than that, slow-motion poise. He watches her walk away, thinks her buttocks really are pleasingly defined. To the individual in treatment, the psychoanalyst may never be completely a person, but then Thomas has always had trouble seeing Anna Stein as an invisible woman.

Then he closes the door and goes back to the computer. His feigned composure is in proportion to his impatience. He waits a few moments, as if delaying reading the e-mail could influence its contents. He is annoyed with himself for this relic of magical thinking, but has long been resigned to the fact that he will never shake it off altogether. He clicks at last. The message is warm, very, and yet does not quite satisfy his hopes. Louise mentions the "very friendly" party and envisions having dinner "really soon" with their mutual friends. Thomas is suddenly afraid he misread her, that she will introduce him to her husband and children, that he will be relegated to the status of a friend or, worse, a friend of theirs. He replies, politely, cautiously, saying he would be delighted to see her again, but for lunch instead, perhaps. Lunch always keeps partners out of the equation. He hopes she gets it. Her answer comes back almost immediately: "Lunch, yes. I'm free tomorrow. Otherwise, not till next week," the message says. Thomas smiles, writes "Where tomorrow?" He clicks. Gust of wind. Barely a minute and the reply comes: "Tomorrow, 1 pm, Café Zimmer at Châtelet."

Then he risks one last e-mail.

"Okay for tomorrow. Do you know, I watched Truffaut's *Stolen Kisses* again yesterday. I'd forgotten the last scene: Claude Jade and Jean-Pierre Léaud are having breakfast after a night spent in each other's arms. They're buttering toast and drinking coffee. He asks for a notebook and a pencil, she gives them to him: he writes a couple of words, tears the page out, folds it and hands it to her. She reads it, takes the notebook, writes something herself, tears the page out like him, folds it and hands it to him. They exchange five or six pages like this, no more, and the audience has no idea what they say. Léaud suddenly takes a bottle opener from the drawer in the table and slips the girl's finger into the circle you fit over the bottle top, as if putting a ring on her. It's one of the loveliest marriage proposals on film. Do you remember that scene? Don't you think it anticipates the miracle of e-mail?"

Gust of wind. The dormant shy guy within him rapidly regrets what he has done. A few minutes later, Louise's reply arrives: "Yes, I do remember that scene from Truffaut. But no relationship with me, I'm already married."

No relationship with me, I'm already married . . . Thomas rereads the sentence, intrigued. All at once the double meaning jumps out at him. The psychoanalyst laughs out loud.

LOUISE

• • •

 ACQUES CHIRAC HAS JUST TAKEN OVER from François
 Mitterrand as president of France, the UN Security
 Council has adopted Resolution 986, known as "Oil for
Food," on Iraq, and Louise Blum, attorney at law, has turned
twenty-five. A tall young woman who is afraid of nothing and
certainly not of having to defend in front of her peers the case
which goes by the absurd title "So What's with the Concierge,
Why Is She on the Stairs?"

The Berryer Conference is a test of eloquence set up by the
Paris bar. In front of a caricature of a chairman and guest of honor
(a writer on this occasion), and confronted with implacably fierce
examiners, young lawyers have to come up with something in-
jected with humor and virtuosity. It is a feat of mental agility.
Places in the competition are highly sought after and only a rare
few are selected: Louise is one of them. She was given her subject—
by drawing lots—half an hour earlier; she quickly devised a plan,
traced her own logic, made a note of some expressions to slip

into her improvisation. The twelve examiners are only too ready to call her out, she has to make it hard for them: Louise wants to conclude on a more serious note (which is traditional), by evoking the vast tower block that is life itself. Because the guest is a writer by profession, she will quote from Georges Perec; mention the tower block in *Life: A User's Manual*; construct an elegant parallel between the stairs, which link the various floors, and law, a house that all men share; establish the connection between domestic and civic order, between the concierge who is the caretaker of a building and the caretaker of the nation's laws.

But first she must get them to laugh. She knows how to do it.

"Mr. Chairman, members of the jury, I know it's something of a national pastime joking about concierges, how surly, lazy, and pathologically inquisitive they are, but I don't want to fall down the elevator shaft of cheap humor at their expense, I mean my father, mother, and sister are in the room. I'm afraid so, Mr. Chairman, as the concierge—her again—would say, I'm still tied to my mother's apron strings. No, I'll be caretaker of my jokes or this concierge will be putting me out with the trash and so will you. What's her name, anyway, Janet or something?"

She makes use of bad puns and a succession of verbal pirouettes, the audience applauds, they drum their feet and whistle. Louise's friends nudge each other: she is off to a good start, at the top of her game.

And she is. Louise holds out like this for a good three minutes. To change tack and win a bit of time, she gives a dramatic flourish of her arms and repeats the question: "Yes, ladies and gentlemen of the jury, what *is* with the concierge, why *is* she on the stairs?"

Then she stops. The tightly calibrated time of the Berryer is punctuated by a pause. The silence lengthens, her friends look at her, start to feel anxious. She has only a few minutes left.

Louise seems to be somewhere else. Her cheeks have gone pale, her blue eyes drained of life. Something is happening, the silence digs even deeper, an uncomfortable feeling settles in the room, this is not a show anymore.

"Yes, of course I know why she is on the stairs."

Her voice has changed, shrugged off any affectation. Louise does not consult her notes, the verve of a defense speech has given way to pure tension. Louise is breathing more quickly, no longer aware of the room:

. . . It is 1942. The concierge is on the stairs and there are two police officers in kepis climbing up behind her

because she's on the stairs, the little sign hanging from the door handle of her room says that the concierge is on the stairs

and they say, Hello ma'am, please could you tell us which floor the Blums live on? Blum as in Leon Blum

and she says, the concierge says, Fourth floor on the left, the Blums live on the left on the fourth floor

yes, that's what the concierge tells them, of course

and it's true that they live on the fourth floor, these Blums

when you're a concierge you answer if a police officer asks you a question, you don't resist

so, sure enough, the police officers ring at the Blums' door

Blum, as everybody knows, is a German word, it means flower

flower as in the Marlene Dietrich song "Sag mir, wo die Blumen sind," where have all the flowers gone?

and that's just what the officers do with the Blums, they pick them like flowers

Good morning, ma'am, good morning, sir

French police

You need to come with us

Yes, it's very early but you'd better bring your stuff, we don't know, this could take a while so the Blums get ready

Hurry please

and the Blums go down the stairs, all four floors with the children

the children

Sarah is seven, Georges ten

Come on, kids, we're going on a journey, don't worry, hey, Georges, you could help your mother with her suitcase, it's too heavy

and hey presto we're on the bus

bus S. It could be S for summer or seaside or sandcastle, but not this time because this one is really bus SS, isn't it

and on the seats next to the Blums are the Sterns and the Cohens, office workers and tailors and barbers, but this wasn't some barber shop quartet, oh no, they were all there. I guess there were some lawyers and magistrates too

forgive me, *former* lawyers and *former* magistrates

that's right, the Blums are now seen in terms of the status that was enacted in 1940

and the judges apply that status, they apply it willingly

a magistrate is like a concierge on the stairs, you just have to ask him and he tells you which floor, straight out. I mean the law's the law

Next case please. Right, let's see what this is. Oh, the Fofana case, yet another one without any papers but does he at least have a lawyer? So sorry, Mr. Fofana, you know what they say, justice may be free but it's not compulsory, ha ha ha

and on to *dura lex sed lex*

through the corridors of the law courts, and let's just have a look at those impressive corridors because at the time they were *Judenfrei*, yes *Judenfrei*, free of Jews, free of Blums

and of course everyone had sworn an oath to Maréchal Pétain

actually that's not true: everyone except Judge Didier. I always forget poor Judge Didier, a legend. Now he was not a concierge, this Judge Didier, he said, No, no, I'm sorry, I won't swear an oath, it's beyond me

he was the only one

but it turns out, ladies and gentlemen, that he made a sacrifice of himself, it was symbolic apparently, there were plenty of others who put up resistance

there really were, really

let's agree on that, can we?

Anyway, in the end everything has one

an end, I mean

and one fine day it all comes to a stop

the good win and the bad lose and that's it, the war's over and everything's just like before, everything, really everything look

lawyers are back pleading their cases in the law courts and the judges are back judging in the law courts too and they're even judging Pétain, the old Maréchal, even him

true, he's old but he still has to be judged to make the point, and who do they come up with to judge him? who do they come up with? nothing but magistrates who swore an oath to him five years earlier. Dear me, that's not pretty, but then *dura lex* once again

and Pétain is condemned to death and then he's granted a pardon

and what about the two police officers you ask. Well, the two police officers are still at the station and one of them, the shorter one, was even made a sergeant. Good morning, Sergeant, oh dear, doesn't anyone salute anymore?

and the bus, that bus S, or SS in fact, it's gone back to the depot and they've repaired the tire because it was giving off smoke, ha! smoke, ha! that's right

and the concierge, she's still on the stairs, yep
but now the Lamberts live on the fourth floor on the left.
Yes, well, the apartment was empty, wasn't it?
  you have to understand the Lamberts have been living there
since '43, on the fourth floor
  water and gas on every floor
  yes, we know where they all are
  the bus, the concierge, the police officers, but tell me, where
are the Blums
  where are they

  Sag mir, wo die Blumen sind?
  Sag mir, wo die Blumen sind?

Louise is almost screeching, her voice cracks and she stops
talking but stays standing. There is absolute silence and the
creak of chairs makes it all the more tangible.
  Louise could step down from the rostrum. But it is not over
yet. She comes right up to the microphone and starts to sing
the Marlene Dietrich song her mother used to sing to her in
German when she was a child, to get her to sleep, she sings very
quietly with a very pure accent:

  Sag mir, wo die Blumen sind *Where have all the flowers gone?*
  Wo sind sie geblieben?   *Long time passing*
  Sag mir, wo die Blumen sind *Where have all the flowers gone?*
  Was ist gescheh'n?   *Long time ago*

Her voice is almost a whisper at first. But with every verse it
grows and becomes louder, filling the dense air, bouncing off
the vaulted ceiling. Louise sings on, with barely a quiver in her
voice, so slight.

Sag mir, wo die Blumen sind	*Where have all the flowers gone?*
Mädchen pflückten sie geschwind	*Gone to young girls every one*
Wann wird man je versteh'n?	*When will they ever learn?*
Wann wird man je versteh'n?	*When will they ever learn?*

Louise inhales and her breathing is amplified by the microphone. Time is suspended for a moment, a scant few seconds. She instinctively goes up a third for the next verse, as her mother used to, as Marlene does:

Sag mir, wo die Mädchen sind	*Where have all the young girls gone?*
Wo sind sie geblieben?	*Long time passing*
Sag mir, wo die Mädchen sind	*Where have all the young girls gone?*
Was ist gescheh'n?	*Long time ago*

No one dares sing along at first. But one voice ventures softly, a man's voice, just humming the tune, then another, and another, more and more of them. A buzzing murmur accompanying her.

Sag mir, wo die Mädchen sind	*Where have all the young girls gone?*
Männer nahmen sie geschwind	*Gone to young men every one*
Wann wird man je versteh'n?	*When will they ever learn?*
Wann wird man je versteh'n?	*When will they ever learn?*
Sag mir, wo die Männer sind	*Where have all the young men gone?*
Wo sind sie geblieben?	*Long time passing*

Sag mir, wo die Männer sind	*Where have all the young men gone?*
Was ist gescheh'n?	*Long time ago*
Sag mir, wo die Männer sind	*Where have all the young men gone?*
Zogen fort, der Krieg beginnt	*Gone as soldiers every one*
Wann wird man je versteh'n?	*When will they ever learn?*
Wann wird man je versteh'n?	*When will they ever learn?*

Louise stops singing, and all the other voices with her. Silence returns, palpable, dense. Somewhere in the room a woman presses a handkerchief over her eyelids, but she is too late, a tear runs down her cheek. She is not Louise's mother. Louise steps down, not hurrying but not waiting for killer questions, which would be customary. There will not be any, they are so dumbstruck, floored, and the chairman—the writer and guest of honor—watches, disconcerted, as this blond little slip of a woman emerges from her dream, dry-eyed and smiling again, and walks toward her friends.

A young man stands up with a loud scrape of his chair, or rather—because he is so tall—he unfolds himself, and he starts to clap, first before anyone else. Some cry "Bravo" but he is crying "Thank you, thank you." The young man's name is Romain, Romain Vidal. He does not yet know Louise, he will meet her properly for the first time later, by chance. He came to the law courts to listen to lawyers jousting, for the fun of it. He does not know it yet, but he is applauding his wife.

As for Louise, the only Jewish thing about her is her name. Her paternal grandfather, Robert Blum, was raised a Jew but had little interest in faith, and married a pretty Breton girl,

Françoise Le Guérec. Louise's grandmother was charming but a bigot, and raised her two sons as Christians: in vain, for Augustin Blum, who doubted anyone could really walk on water or multiply loaves of bread, gave Louise and her sister a perfectly secular upbringing. But this grandfather whose name she bears, this Jew originally from Berlin who survived the roundup at the Vel d'Hiv[2] and died when she was only eight, has always fascinated Louise. Her performance at the Berryer would be the final eruption of his identity.

2. The Velodrôme d'Hiver was a cycling stadium in Paris where, in July 1942, thirteen thousand Jews were rounded up, to be sent to the camp at Drancy.

YVES

· · ·

T AGE THREE, little Yves could read. The child was looking over his grandfather's shoulder when he asked what the word "Kennedy" meant (the article was about the revolution in Cuba). The grandfather immediately picked up the telephone to call his daughter: "You'll never believe this! Your little Yves! He can read!"

At every important family gathering, Yves, eyes lowered and cheeks flushed with embarrassment, had to suffer the retelling of this "Kennedy affair," glorified by his triumphantly proud mother.

Learning to write took him longer. He made few mistakes, but his writing was untidy, his letters irregular. From the age of twelve, Yves always kept a pad in his pocket. He would jot down a sentence overheard, a few lines of poetry, a new word that intrigued him. This urge to copy things down would never leave him. Soon afterward he kept notebooks, writing poems and short stories in them. It was only at thirty-two, the day after his daughter Julie was born, that he threw away the boxes filled with his early writings. No feeling of regret ever materialized.

Yves Janvier is walking through Paris with a new notebook in his pocket. The one he has now is light and hardcover, in black leather. This model usually lasts a couple of months. As he crosses the Île de la Cité and the flower market, he writes a few cramped, uneven, sloping lines, which he will have trouble reading when he comes to type them on the computer:

A passerby stops beside a painter in the Fontainebleau forest. The painter is Jean-Baptiste Corot. Find a date: 1855, 1860? The passerby looks at the painting, recognizes the fir trees in it, the silver birches, but, in the view before him, he cannot see the pond with twinkling water from the middle of the painting. He asks Corot where the pond is. Corot doesn't even turn around but replies: "It's behind me." A parable. But about what? Maybe just tell it without relating it to anything.

His notebook contains other, more incomprehensible notes. "Jupiter's moons. Twelve. Some can be seen with the naked eye." And "Being on the crest. Climbing up from the valley to be on the crest. No interest in the mountain per se."

A few pages earlier, Yves Janvier also noted:

"What is it about the rain I like so much?"

"Why have I always hated having my picture taken?"

"We talk about overwhelmed and underwhelmed, but is anyone ever whelmed?"

"The left cerebral hemisphere controls speech (Paul Broca)."

"Abkhazian dominoes, the only game of dominoes where, if you can't play, you are allowed to pick up a domino that's already on the board."

It will all be useful, perhaps.

It is worth listing the things that were sources of interest to Yves at one point or another: as with many children, it was dinosaurs that first fascinated him. His parents bought illustrated books for him, books "for his age group," but he soon wanted more advanced material. When, aged nine, he saw an artist's drawing in a newspaper, he was irritated by the anachronism of a pterodactyl wheeling above a herd of plateosauruses. Had he been abandoned in the middle of the Jurassic period he would easily have distinguished the very peaceful barosaurus from the no less placid camarasaurus. His family believed this was the start of a lasting interest, perhaps even a vocation, but after a visit to the botanical gardens, he turned his attention to carnivorous plants. Yves was immediately treated to his own hothouse, where for six months he fed a row of Venus flytraps on midges and crickets. Then came his hieroglyphics, cartouches, and reed pens period.

Yves's curiosity is still alert, insatiable. Over the years he has learned a great deal about Ethiopian wildlife, prehistoric population migration, the evolution of sentence structure in Flaubert's work, the harmonics of baroque scales, the early centuries of the Catholic Church, the poetry of the Grands Rhétoriqueurs, successive theories of color, the effects of gravitational pull close to black holes, the history of bebop and after-hours jazz, the logic of symbiotic relationships, unified theories of the universe, and even how to solve differential equations. Each area of research has him in its clutches for a few weeks, sometimes months. He buys books that give an overview, until he is irritated at having to reread in one a concept already explained in another, then he launches into understanding more detailed points. He turns his back on a subject once he has learned a great deal about it, and a new passion takes possession of him. He forgets a huge amount, he realizes that. So, anything he wants to use, such as Broca's area which controls speech, he notes down so as not to forget, or rather so he can forget it. What he does remember is too often anecdotal. But then what is knowledge for a lot of people if not an organized accumulation of anecdotes?

Occasionally, if an inquisitive stranger—a taxi driver, a provincial hairdresser, a fellow passenger on a train—should ask him about his life, Yves invents a profession and constructs a life for himself, with the perfect impunity of anonymity. He fictionalizes out of courtesy, almost out of discretion. It is an opportunity to inventory his areas of expertise, to structure them for the sake of civilized conversation. He even tries to inspire the person he is talking to, coloring his voice with a genuine passion. Just for as long as it takes for the taxi to reach Place d'Italie—by the time they pass the rue Montmartre, he is one of Europe's leading authorities on cryptobiosis in tardigrades.

"On what in what?" says the driver.

"Cryptobiosis in tardigrades. Tardigrades are tiny invertebrates, no bigger than a pinhead. They can expel all the water from their bodies to withstand extreme temperatures in the Antarctic: that's what cryptobiosis is. They can survive in that state for many years, centuries even. I've been studying them for twenty-two years now."

"Are we paying you for this out of our taxes?" the driver asks anxiously.

"Oh . . . I see . . . ," says Yves. Then his voice becomes more crisp, as would be appropriate for an offended researcher: "But, you see, if you're told you have cancer, which I hope you aren't, but let's say you are, and I work out how to keep you alive in a frozen state until a cure is found for this bastard cancer, you won't mind funding my little salary all the years I've been studying tardigrades."

"Yeah, okay, true enough," admits the now reassured, taxpaying driver. "So what are they called, tradigrades, did you say?"

"Tardi. Tardigrades. And cryptobiosis."

"Cryptobosis," the driver repeats meekly, nodding.

"Biosis. Like biology."

Victory by default.

Sometimes the game requires judgment. At a barber's in Rennes, he once said he was a museum curator, adding, "At the Space Museum."

"Really? The Space Museum? I don't believe it," said the customer next to him. "That's fantastic."

Unlucky: the guy turned out to be an amateur astronomer who had been subscribing to *Air and Cosmos* magazine "from the age of twelve," and all through his childhood—he admitted with child-in-a-candy-store enthusiasm—he built models of space shuttles, space capsules, and launchers: "My favorites were the Soyuz-U, they were the real McCoy." He has the best one in his living room. It is on a scale of one to twenty-four but still measures seven feet; he used a candle to reproduce the fuel burns on the propulsion nozzles.

"It pisses my wife off but the kids love it."

Yves lets him talk, knowing from experience this is an infallible tactic: the first thing an amateur meeting a specialist wants to do is display his knowledge, be sent off with flying colors. This man, Yves realizes instinctively, knows a lot more than he does on the subject. So he cautiously restricts the conversation to a subject he has mastered, claiming there is an upcoming exhibition: the life of Werner von Braun, the ex-Nazi scientist who ran NASA during the space race. He mentions the CIA's Operation Paperback, in which they exfiltrated war criminals to serve the needs of the Cold War, and talks about the Dora work camp where von Braun was a particularly zealous *Obersturmführer*. Yves never hesitates, confidently coining the names of "that crook" von Braun's collaborators: Gustav Jung and Friedrich Hofmannsthal. The surnames may be fakes, borrowed from other fields, but all the anecdotes Yves relates are real: that is his elegance as a liar. He holds out like this for ten minutes, easily. Yves is grateful for having short straight hair, the barber has already finished cutting it.

"Perhaps I could come and see you at the museum?" asks the *Air and Cosmos* subscriber.

Yves feels awkward, crestfallen, as he always does when he has to leave the fiction and turn to real deception. Misleading such a charming man ruins the pleasure of inventing another life for himself. He finds an escape route.

Yves is not a pathological liar. He simply regrets that, in his teens, no single passion swept aside all the others and overtook him completely. He became neither a biologist nor a theologian, astronomer, or historian. Yves is a writer. He makes things up unashamedly partly because admitting what he does to a stranger always results in an intrigued "And what have you written?" inevitably followed by the perennial "Sorry, I haven't read it."

A writer. It took him a long time to call himself one, but he lives with words and ended up living off them, not as comfortably as he would like, but a good deal better than he had suspected. His editors reassure him: "You have readers, but you haven't yet found your true readership." Yves is not sure he is the type that has a true readership.

Yves is a writer because he could not write "infinite tender-ness," "life's journey," or "hopelessly in love" without feeling ashamed. From time to time he lets slip a "sleeping heavily," "quick as a flash," and "scribbled in haste," and is very upset when he spots the cliché once the book is published. He often uses superfluous commas too, then exterminates them merci-lessly. He has read too much not to know that writing well means writing badly, as someone once said. He wishes every sentence spilled out of him, surprised him, and that the sur-prise would never lose its sparkle. He reads over his work, ex-asperated to find mannerisms in his writing; then he erases the seductive ring it had, the elegant turn of phrase, he tracks down the literary pleonasm and destroys the ternary rhythm that comes to him naturally. Sometimes there is nothing left of the first draft, except perhaps its bare bones. In trying to grasp the kernel of life, Giacometti constantly stripped clay from his iron framework. The language Yves Janvier pummels at is his enemy, he knows it is too exotic and too intimate. His words try to depict real things, like flagstones covering beaten earth: but, in places, rebellious weeds poke through. He could go on deleting and reworking forever. He is hoping for a miracle, for absolute grace, and senses it only in other people's work. He is not sure whether this dissatisfaction is proof of being an artist.

His brief meeting with Anna Stein was something he wanted to write about that same evening. It was simple: a young woman at a party, where he only meant to stop by, talks about the in-cest taboo, about the French Revolution, Freud, and the law. He goes over and listens. And is immediately attracted to her. Some people are staying for dinner, she is one of them. He fol-lows them, follows her. She is still talking, about childhood, ill-ness, death, she gets to him even more. It is so straightforward.

How to describe the beginnings of love? That eternal question. Of course, "eternal question" is a cliché.

But he did not give up. At first he struggled at length over every word, every sentence. When the page was finally covered with writing, a sort of poetry with a set, musical rhythm had written itself beneath his fingers, a poetry in which he spoke to her, intimate, familiar. It did not surprise him. The form was so self-evident it carried him along.

THOMAS AND YVES

. . .

*T*HOMAS LE GALL IS CURIOUS about Louise Blum, curious
and in a hurry.

The moment the door to his office is closed, he calls the
friend who invited him to Sammy's dinner, thanking him yet
again. Feigning detachment, he tries to find out more about
Louise. He clearly is not discreet enough: he earns an ironic
laugh.

"Are you interested in Romain Vidal's wife, then?"

Thomas does not deny it, but changes the subject. The
name Romain Vidal means something to him. In a few clicks,
he knows almost everything about Louise Blum's husband: a
doctor of biology and linguistics, he is a respected researcher
and a shameless popularizer with over two hundred thousand
references on the Internet. Thomas types in his own name. Ten
times fewer, nothing to show off about. Not forgetting that there
are also Thomas Le Galls who are pharmacists in Saint-Malo

or headmasters of elementary schools in Quebec . . . Yves Jan-vier, how many of them? Thirty-five thousand times. Thomas switches off his computer and closes up.

In the bookstore on the Place de la Contrescarpe, there are piles of copies of Yves Janvier's *Two-Leaf Clover*. He asks the proprietor about it, and the total lack of conviction in the man's voice—"It's not bad"—proves he knows absolutely noth-ing about it. Thomas buys one and, because the sun is shining, because it is still warm, he sits out on a terrace facing the foun-tain on the rue Mouffetard and orders a cup of coffee.

Janvier, on the back cover, is not smiling at the photographer. The face does have its curves but long vertical creases on the cheeks and forehead disrupt its softness. The fair hair grows more scant over the forehead. The man's jaw is a blend of tough and gentle. Thomas would never have guessed he was Anna's type.

Two-Leaf Clover is a far cry from a Russian novel. At barely a hundred pages, it is more a novella, clipping along energeti-cally, comprising twelve short chapters. He finishes it in less than an hour. Anna Stein summarized the premise well: under intermittent Celtic rain, a man is confronted with a young mis-tress's cold shoulder and the casual hostility of a rented Toyota. Sickly sweet cruelty, tidy economy of expression, moments of linguistic invention. Is it the sunlight, the Indian sum-mer, the bittersweetness of his coffee? This slender book has dropped him straight into friendly territory. If Louise could be Anna's cousin, then Yves—he can see it himself—could easily be Thomas's own brother. Of course, they do have Anna in common. Getting to know Janvier better hardly strikes him as intrusive. Lacan never hesitated to make contact with his patients' partners or even their mothers. That was still more extreme, but is far from a valid argument.

Thomas puts down his glasses—he and his glasses have been inseparable for several years. Philosophy may aim to domesticate death, but farsightedness is there every day to reinforce it. He looks at the fine tortoiseshell frame, the light reflected in the lenses, not realizing he is inadvertently grimacing.

Thomas stands up and gazes briefly at the water spilling from the fountain. His cell phone rings and the screen shows a woman's name, an old girlfriend with whom, some evenings, he likes to be a cuddling companion. A "colorful friendship" is the way they describe their intimacy. It sounds a lot better than colorless love. Thomas answers.

YVES AND ARIANE

• • •

*Y*VES JANVIER IS STILL SLIM, the tall sporty teenager he once was lives on in the way he moves. He runs across the Quai des Grands-Augustins, and, at fifty, could pass for a young man, although he is furious to be out of breath. His temples have been gray for a long time, but there has been a rebellious swirl through his hair ever since childhood, and it gives him a rakish, Monsieur Hulot look.

Yves is walking across Paris because he is leaving Ariane. He realizes that he left her a long time ago now, but she does not know it because nothing about them has changed on the surface. They eat, live, and sleep together, do not make love any less frequently because they had come to do it so little, and they still hold hands with genuine tenderness.

Janvier met Ariane three years earlier at a book fair in Nantes where he was being asked to sign pitifully few books and growing very bored, without actually succumbing to the temptation of getting drunk on sparkling wine. A pretty girl with brown hair and dark skin handed him a book that was a good ten years old and said: "For Ariane." He immediately turned to the inside cover and wrote, rather provocatively: "For Ariane, who knows that a phone call can save a life." It was stupid as could be, a bit crass even, but she smiled kindly and slipped away. In the train on the way back to Paris, she was having a cup of coffee in the dining car. When she saw him, she smiled and pretended to pick up a phone, murmured "Hello," and mimed a conversation. He apologized for his dedication, blaming the excess of sparkling white. They had dinner together that same evening, and she decided to spend the night at his place. They were both free.

She liked the gray of his eyes, the misleading impression he gave of being bored all the time, and the way he smiled fleetingly in public, as if he only shared his smiles with her. She was radiant and graceful, and Yves Janvier was seduced by this combination of fragility and assurance so fundamental to the young. Because yes, she was young, and often seemed even younger. To the tactless waiter who once asked: "And what would your daughter like?" Ariane retorted: "Please, we've been married ten years." Another time she was so irritated she even went as far as "for twenty years." Yves burst out laughing, and so did she.

Fairly soon, simply and easily, Ariane moved in with Janvier. She did not have much furniture, not many clothes. He suggested she should sublet her one-bedroom apartment, she offered to pay half his rent, they shared the bills. Janvier was worried about tensions with his thirteen-year-old daughter Julie, but Ariane succeeded in making her more than a friend, an ally. "This time, I beg you, don't lose her," Julie would say happily to her father.

Ariane still had some nocturnal social habits from her student years, and Janvier did not want to crush them. The friends she went out with at night were as young as she was. Young— he was not jealous of them for that: it meant he did not have to pretend to be, when he was with her. Yves worked in the evenings, until late, and they met up even later, well into the night. Life was good, happy, easy. People envied them.

Yves is going to break up with Ariane. He thinks that if he had not met Anna Stein, it could have lasted a long time. Unless he met Anna Stein because it could not go on any longer. He is tickled by the balance between these two sentences, and writes them in his notebook.

He does not know what to expect from Anna Stein. He could not even describe her properly, the shape of her face, the color of her eyes. She is still just a feeling, but this feeling runs deep, and no longer leaves room for doubt. He had forgotten that painful, acutely intimate disruption, thought its source had run dry, blamed experience which makes everything lose its savor, or, worse, the years ticking by: they did not come into it, then. He finds this both reassuring and unsettling. He had so many tender moments with Ariane. So why did not one of them produce this burning sensation? He said "I love you" to her a thousand times. How does he now know he was lying to her every time? Yves is going to leave Ariane, and he is ashamed of that sugary warmth called fondness, ashamed of the sadness he will have to fake, ashamed of this explosive new enthusiasm he will have to hide.

Ariane is waiting for him in a café in the rue Monsieur Le Prince, she is drinking hot chocolate and reading. Before she sees him, Yves studies her. She really is very pretty, perhaps more so than Anna Stein in many people's eyes. Gentler, too, more cheerful, he can tell already. He even knows that he will always think of her, of them, nostalgically, that he will soon miss this tender sense of peace, and knows he will never dare admit this regret to her later. But Anna Stein has captivated him, dazzled him, and Yves is not putting up a fight, he wants to be exposed to this blissful onslaught, he wants to experience the vertiginous fall once more, having given up hope of finding it again.

THOMAS AND LOUISE

. . .

THOMAS DOES NOT LIKE THE ZIMMER HOTEL. He has not set foot in the place for ten years, but nothing has changed. Still too much velvet, too much red, too much carpeting. And too many cars on the Place du Châtelet. All the same, he does like not feeling at home: having to confront those rococo chairs and sofas gives him a boost. He is far too early, by almost half an hour, without meaning to be. Ten years ago, he would have spent the time browsing the *bouquiniste* stalls for secondhand books, or dropped in to look at stick insects and boa constrictors at the zoo. But his youthful curiosity has been dulled, and any reenactment would taint the experience with nostalgia. All the same, if Louise would like to, he will take her to shudder at the reptiles and tarantulas, he will tell her about the Galápagos marine iguana, the only animal whose skeleton shrinks when food is in short supply.

Thomas wants to sit at the far end of the room but he spots her at a table, with a cup of tea. She is wearing a floaty dress, very 1930s, with calculated elegance. This fearless way of wearing an outfit is something he has noticed in Anna Stein too. It demonstrates coquettishness, but then he is not averse to the idea that Louise might be just that, coquettish. She is typing away on a laptop, talking into an earpiece over her temple, it is a business conversation. He wants to move away but she smiles at him and gestures for him to sit down.

"I'm so sorry, your honor, I'm going into a hearing right now . . . We can talk about my client tomorrow, if that's all right with you. Without fail . . . and I'll see you on Tuesday, yes."

Louise hangs up, Thomas studies her in the harsh sunlight, makes out for the first time the fine crow's-feet around her eyes, the brown shadows under them, the hundreds of silvery threads in the blond of her hair.

"Hello. You're good at lying."

"I'm at the right school . . . It wasn't me, sir . . . I didn't steal anything, I didn't kill anyone, I didn't rape her. I meet liars every day . . ."

"An analyst spends his life with liars too, liars who know they're lying, and sincere liars who don't. Everyone lies."

When Louise Blum thinks, she crinkles her brow, and Thomas is charmed by this vertical furrow.

"No, not everyone. Not my husband."

"Really . . . that's not normal at all. He should have analysis."

"But that's the way he is, he doesn't lie. Romain is a scientist, and scientists don't lie."

"Romain Vidal, I know. He's very well known."

"Very well known? Well . . . quite."

Louise does not say anything else. She puts away her papers and turns off the computer, then makes a few last notes in a notebook, in pretty, fluid writing. The sun gives her a blond halo, her eyes have a golden glint. He finds her so radiant, so wonderful that he immediately recognizes this feeling of exultation. Stendhal only too accurately defined that crystallization, the moment when the lover—Thomas does not know the sentence by heart—"draws from everything in sight the discovery that the object of his love has new perfections," in the same way that, in just a few months, a tree that falls into the Salzburg salt mines is covered, every last twig, in "dazzling shifting diamonds." But just because Thomas understands the whys and wherefores, Louise does not glitter any the less.

"I couldn't have hoped to see you again so soon," he says with that courage peculiar to the shy.

"I wanted a free session."

"There is no such thing as a free session. It's like with meals. There's always a price to pay."

"I'll pay. So, tell me. How do you become a psychoanalyst?"

"Oh. Do you want the quick answer or the long answer? The long one takes five years."

Louise wants the quick answer. Thomas explains the Jardin du Luxembourg, his pointless dilettantism, his rejection of self, the violent intrusion of death with Piette's suicide, his metamorphosis, how he met the mother of his two daughters, and the sudden fear, when he was thirty and finishing med school, that he had no genuine longings, that he was nothing. He talks for quite a while, openly. He has already said it all, to a different person, in a different way.

"I had no idea what I really wanted. There was a wall in front of me. My life was behind that wall. I started in analysis, to live. It took time. It was a big wall."

"And now?"

"The wall's still there, but I know how to get through it, sometimes."

Louise listens to him, looks at him. Thomas's face is gentle, serene. His dark eyes and deep voice soothe her. She so rarely feels soothed, so rarely feels secure.

"Thomas . . . this morning, I was just leaving, and Romain didn't ask me anything . . . but, even so, I told him I was having lunch with a client."

She picks up her cup, puts it back down, waits, but Thomas never asks his question. She raises her eyebrows, tilts her head.

"Aren't you going to ask me why? I thought you were a psychoanalyst?"

"That's just the point: it's not up to the analyst to say anything."

Rather earnestly, Thomas takes a notebook and felt-tip pen from his pocket, and carefully writes the date at the top of the page.

"Mrs. Blum, I never charge for the first session. We can set the rate for our meetings later. Let's start again. I'm listening."

"Good. So, first of all I answered a question Romain didn't ask. That surprised me. Then, I made you a client. I've been thinking about it all morning. In ten years I've never lied to Romain."

She stops talking. Thomas watches her. She has a bead of sweat on the tip of her nose, her eyes are focused on the dregs of Thomas's coffee.

"You see, I must have lied because I feel guilty about seeing you. Of course, I could have not told Romain anything, or told him all about you and the dinner the other night. But it would only have been to make me feel less guilty."

She pauses, takes a sip of tea.

"But mostly, confessing to him would have been like trying to protect myself from how much I wanted to be here, and even from the pleasure I would get out of it. When, in fact, that was something I didn't want to do."

The bead of sweat slips off her nose. Louise is slightly short of breath.

"I'm completely nuts talking to you like this. In fact, I must seem . . ."

"No. You don't seem anything at all."

"In fact, I've never dared behave like this. It must be some kind of analyst effect."

She looks at him, her eyes are shining, but not with mischief. Thomas really has been taking notes.

"So? What do you think, Doctor?"

"Mrs. Blum, the analyst can confirm that you very frequently use the expression 'in fact.' He suspects this is some form of denial. Precisely because it is not a 'fact,' it is an unconscious admission of a fantasy."

Louise makes a face, rather prettily.

"But," he is quick to clarify, "the analyst has restricted himself to collating fragments of speech which may prove relevant—or not. As for the man, he . . ."

"Yes? The man?"

"I've been dying to see you since I left you that evening. I came up with other strategies in case you weren't free today, and was trying to find some pretext in case you didn't agree to see me. You know everything. And, to be honest . . ."

"Yes?"

"I haven't had anyone to lie to in the morning for a long time. Mind you, I don't lie either."

"I wouldn't want you to . . . I'm not sure I like 'agree to see me' . . . I'm not that . . ."

"You don't have to justify anything."

Louise stands up, puts on her coat, and turns up the collar.

"Thomas, I'm not hungry at all. It's half past one, I have a hearing at the law courts at three-thirty. And it's a beautiful day."

"Would you like to go to the zoo? Did you know that when iguanas can't get enough food, their skeletons shrink?"

"So the skeleton is to the iguana what the brain is to man, then?"

"Let's put it like that."

Thomas is delighted to find he is quite devoid of malice or calculation. He finds the Galápagos marine iguana interesting again. They leave, walk a few steps, and he takes her hand which she has left by her side. Under the first awning—who leads whom?—they kiss. He finds her lips taste of ripe blackberries and licorice, familiar; she recognizes his aftershave, Romain used to wear the same one, a long time ago.

The kiss goes on a long time, they are offering themselves to each other, unhurriedly, Thomas holds her to him. Louise pulls away, whispers something in his ear. Thomas smiles, shakes his head. An empty taxi approaches. Thomas hails it. The iguanas can wait behind their glass.

ANNA AND YVES

· · ·

*Y*ves. Yves. However many times Anna Stein says it, she cannot find anything attractive about the name. She would have preferred something else, not so unfashionable, less dated. A Lucas, a Serge, or a David. Something less "French," more international, more cosmopolitan, a name that did not smell of the earth beneath our feet: I can't get used to the idea that he's called Yves, the idea that I'm in love with an Yves.

Yves, then. She has called him three times already, for reasons that are only too obviously excuses. Saying "Hello, Yves?" is exhilarating. That in itself is an adventure, feeling the breath leave her as she pronounces his name. She likes his voice, on the telephone, how he holds on to every word for a moment, slowing the pace, she is unsettled by the way he seems to struggle to find the words, the way he concentrates and hesitates. She likes his intonation, his timbre, his almost writerly turn of phrase. She sees an intensity in this, and that intensity cuts right through her, she reads a spirit of life into it, something he carries in him, not something she could manifest. This man owes her nothing. He did not wait for her to get on with his life, and the foreign territory of a man's past in which she does not exist draws her in like a whirlwind.

Until now, Anna only knew one Yves: Yves Beaudouin, her manager. Usually when she came home from work she would simply tell Stan: Yves this, Yves that. But yesterday she added his last name: Yves Beaudouin, as if this specifying were needed.

Stan was taken aback and asked his wife, rather sardonically, "Is there another one?"

Anna looked at him, frowned, feigned bafflement.

"Another Yves," he explained.

She concealed her embarrassment, smiled: "You're so silly."

Of course an answer like that was an admission. She would have liked it if Stan had guessed and pressed the matter, but because he did not notice, because he refused yet again to open his eyes, her guilt feels correspondingly slighter, and now look, he's even more guilty than she is.

ROMAIN

• • •

*T*HERE IS A SIGN ON THE TALL OAK DOOR in the lobby of
the School of Medicine. It has an arrow pointing the
way to a study seminar on "The Genetics of Language" and
adds: OPENING CONFERENCE BY PROF. ROMAIN VIDAL. 4–6
PM. The Linnaean Auditorium no longer has a single seat free,
and the age of the audience proves, as is rarely the case, that
it includes more lecturers than students. There are two men
on the stage chatting and smiling. One can only imagine they
are united by some complicity of learning, so utterly are they
separated by physical appearance. The first—almost a giant,
barely forty, wearing a white shirt and faded jeans—is checking
the wires connected to his laptop. The older, chubbier man, in
a blue suit with a salmon pink tie, is tapping the microphone.

"Hello, can you hear me? Please take your seats, there are
still a few places at the front, please use them . . . As director
of the Department of Medicine at Paris V University, it is my

privilege to welcome a friend, Dr. Romain Vidal. He is the first contributor in our cycle of lectures. Romain will speak in French, but if you use the headphones supplied at the door, there will be a simultaneous translation into English. Romain directs Unit 468 of the National Institute for Health and Medical Research, which deals with 'Language and the Nervous System.' He teaches biological chemistry at Paris V University and was professor of genetics at Princeton for several years. Some of you still know Romain Vidal for his reader-friendly book, cowritten with the Nobel Prize winner John Vermont, on proto-language in animals, *Animals That Speak.*"

". . . *That Speak?*" Romain lets his voice hang in the air, to indicate the question mark.

"*Animals That Speak?* Sorry, Romain. Was my accent any good, at least?"

Romain Vidal's pout provokes some chuckling.

"I see . . . I'd better leave you to speak, then."

Romain nods his head, amicably. He stays standing, checks his microphone. His voice is clear with precise diction, professional.

Thank you, Jacques, for that brief introduction. I'm very happy to be back where I studied cellular biology twenty years ago. So, this inaugural conference goes by the title "Keys to the Genetics of Language." I'm going to try, in the hour I have, to share the extent of my findings with you. In order to do that, I need first to give you an acceptable definition of language, then to ask you to consider its role in the evolution of mankind, before looking into how it has mutated and changed, from three different points of view: genetic, evolutionary, and linguistic. Finally, I shall outline the position on what hopes there are in the field of gene therapy. To conclude, I will explain why I have high hopes of one day holding a conversation with Darwin. Darwin is my daughters' cat. When you leave this room, I hope you will know more than when you came in. Which will make you all the more ignorant, given that, as someone—I can't remember who, oh, actually, I can, it was Henri Michaux—so rightly said, "All knowledge creates new ignorance."

The audience smiles. Romain Vidal has earned a reputation as an entertaining speaker who respects his audience. It is also his own recipe for avoiding boredom. The hesitation on Michaux was partly a ploy. Louise taught him, years ago now, a lawyer's trick: "If you want to keep their attention, darling, make them laugh from time to time, and quote Flaubert, just like that, as if it was nothing, but always make it relevant. Or Dostoevsky, or Borges. You can't invent this stuff, my love, you have to work really hard to make it look natural. They'll never forget you. Even if they don't remember a word of the case you made, they'll remember the sentence from Flaubert. And never deliver the same author twice to the same people. They would take far too much pleasure in saying you rambled."

Romain continues:

We have always been preoccupied with the question of animal language. We say "animal," "language," "we," and each of these words supports a concept. In the book of Genesis, only Adam can name things. But do animals name things too? If they do, then man is not alone in speaking, he is not alone in deciphering the world. What new position does he hold in the world then? Advances in biology give rise to ethical, philosophical, and political questions. The genetics of language pose a phenomenal number of these questions. I shall be covering birds, primates, and dolphins, but first I'd like to talk about man, because man constitutes the most straightforward subject—paradoxically, given that his language is the most evolved. It would be extremely difficult for us to identify language problems in animals, but there must be chimpanzees with stammers out there, and dyslexic dolphins . . .

"After a joke," Louise also advised, "never play up to it. Don't pause, take a sip of water instead." Romain brings the glass to his lips.

Some people have pathological problems with speech. This sort of "specific language distortion" is not related to mental handicaps. Toward the end of the twentieth century, the genealogy of a Pakistani family from the East End of London was studied in detail because several members of the family had trouble with articulation, with constructing coherent sentences, sometimes even with identifying sounds. The researchers managed to identify a deformity on a short section of chromosome 7, the gene FOXP2. FOXP2, which stands for Forkhead box P 2, is a protein characterized by a sequence of about a hundred amino acids connected to the DNA in a butterfly-shaped pattern. On this slide you can see highlighted in red the site of the mutation on exon 14. The guanine in one of the nucleotides is replaced by adenanine.

This FOXP2 gene plays a decisive role in the production of language in all animals. It acts like the conductor of an orchestra when the neural pathways are being laid down during embryo development. A "knockout" mouse (one that has been genetically modified) in which FOXP2 has been altered does not squeak like a normal mouse but almost like a bat, in the ultrasonic range. I'd like to refer you to the work of the team comprising Shu, Morrisey, Buxbaum et al. This gene also codes the swallowing process, tongue movements, etc.

In *Homo erectus*, FOXP2 mutated radically some two hundred thousand years ago. In other words, shortly before the advent of the Neanderthals and ourselves, the Cro-Magnons, *Homo sapiens*. This FOXP2 mutation is found in both types of *Homo*. It supports presumptions of a common ancestor, but that's a whole other debate. So language appears less as a tool than as an organ. An organ which requires an indispensable process of apprenticeship. Mastering it goes hand in hand with the development of the cervical lobes: the brain is then arranged around language just as language structures the brain. That's why we cannot acquire a so-called mother tongue after the age of six . . . but I'm not here to talk about the ontogenesis of language, other contributors will cover that, and I don't want to encroach on their territory. In any event, I'm not interested in distinguishing between the acquired and the innate, but in knowing, first, when in the genetic history of a primate population the mutation facilitating speech occurred, and second, at what point in an individual's development the neural connections that make language possible are established. We are still waiting for breakthroughs in the ontogenesis and phylogenesis of language.

Let's say that, just as there was a proto-eye before the eye and a proto-hand before the hand, there was also a proto-language before language. A language of a few dozen words, but one, I fear, we know nothing about, because language doesn't fossilize very well. I have nothing against Plato when he explains in his *Cratylus* that words appear in relation to natural sounds. Here I'd like to refer you to Jakobson's famous article: yes, "mama" is almost certainly a universal that is systematically reinvented for the simple reason that *ma* is the first sound a baby can make. I'm also happy to accept that the word "tiger" comes from the roar of that *grr*. And I won't devote my energies to disputing

Merritt Ruehlen's affirmations about mother tongue, the proto-nostratic language, although, to my mind, archeolinguistics is far too speculative, except for writing poems.

I will confine myself to one certainty: this proto-language must have conferred a decisive competitive advantage. Of course, there is the utilitarian vision: language means you can warn the group of unseen danger, tell them where to find food, and share experience. But I am even more keen on what I shall call the "litterarist" hypothesis: in social primates such as *Homo neanderthalensis* and *Homo sapiens*, language means first and foremost being able to tell a story. The new tradition says: "Don't kill your neighbor because someone once did that and you just listen to what happened to them." Myth then reinforces the group's social cohesion and acts as a counterbalance to the effects of intelligence and individual self-interest. Not forgetting that, according to some evolutionists, language constitutes an advantage in the sexual realm: a female would choose a male who masters language over one with a more impressive physique: Rimbaud rather than Rambo. This theory is very popular with academics, particularly those not endowed with much muscle.

Romain the svelte turns toward the pudgy Jacques; his schoolboy joke makes the audience laugh. It works every time.

Romain will not reveal how, ten years earlier, he spent his first evening with Louise stammering and stuttering while his future wife—perfectly at ease and perfectly in control of her emotions—affectionately made fun of him, even then. The young academic did not win her, it was more she who chose him. For his natural decency, for the almost naive purity in the way he looked at her, and for his acute intelligence made all the more dazzling by his terrible gaucheness. But Louise very quickly realized that this peculiar difficulty with words that initially seduced her would end up exasperating her. Turning Romain into an incomparable orator struck her as a worthy challenge. And he soon became one. But his newfound assurance did not draw solely on exercises in diction and the quality of his notes. It owed much more to the pride he felt in being the man whom Louise Blum allowed to walk beside her in the street.

"Now I would like to cut to the quick of the subject . . ." Romain goes on.

When, an hour and ten minutes later, with that appropriate runover on time, the speaker stops talking and invites his audience to contribute in a discussion, there is one man in the back row of the Linnaean Auditorium who has not taken a single note. When the question-and-answer session begins, the man does not ask any questions either, even though, like all psychoanalysts, he would have liked to hear the word "subconscious" pronounced at some point in this conference on the cognitive sciences.

Thomas Le Gall has not taken his eyes off Romain Vidal for a moment, though. This is the man who wakes every morning beside Louise Blum, the woman he is falling in love with, and whom he has just made love to for the first time. Romain Vidal is not his rival, because no one ever has a rival. Thomas had no urge to confront the image of "the husband." He wanted to see the man that Louise Blum had loved and still loved, and also, perhaps, wanted to put his own feelings to the test. Thomas feels the beginnings of sympathy for this great tall boy whose secret shyness he can see, whose fluid logical train of thought he admires, and whose friendship he knows with regret he can never have.

ANNA AND STAN

. . .

*I*T HAD BEEN SUCH A HOT SUMMER. Anna and Stan spent it near Grignan, in the house they rented every year. The heat wave sent statistics through the roof. Twice as many forest fires, homicides, multiple pileups, and old people dying in hospices. The drought affected sixty regional *départements*. There was a ban on filling swimming pools, and those that were filled had to act as reservoirs for the fire department. On the radio and in bistros, all the talk was of global warming. When Karl and Lea sat down in the car, they squealed because the seats were so hot. Anna ran a damp sponge over the plastic surfaces to cool them, and the children begged to have the air conditioning on but kept the windows open.

They were bored. They devoted the morning to making a list of things they needed to buy, went into town to buy them, and had a coffee on the town square, then the temperature started to rise and they went back to the house. They ate lunch, cleared the table, and did the dishes before the ants invaded. It was too hot to have a siesta. Karl and Lea squabbled constantly to fill the time.

There were wasps. Stan made a trap by cutting open an Evian bottle and putting very sugary wine into it. They soon came to die in there, dozens of them. Anna could not bear to see her children entertained by their endless paddling, the hours they took to die. Particularly Karl, who called her in a state of great excitement every time a new victim ventured into the fatal opening. She did not recognize her own son in this cruel delight. He was the one who, with morbid fascination, emptied out the insect juice at the bottom of the garden every morning.

There was also the pool. It was unfit for use before five o'clock in the afternoon, when the sun dived behind the old farmhouse. The children watched the line of shadow advance very slowly across the blazing hot paving stones, as if watching the progress of a column of ants.

"Mommy, mommy," they cried every minute, "another stone in the shade!"

"Great!" Anna replied, from the sofa in the living room.

In the evening, when the children were in bed, Stan and Anna stayed out on the terrace to make the most of a coolness that never materialized. Stan rubbed the back of his wife's neck, she ducked away from his touch. It was so hot, or she was reading, or she didn't feel like it. One night, Stan took her. She consented despite how clammy their bodies were, and even reached orgasm; she fell asleep right away.

At the end of August they packed their bags and went home to Paris. On the trip back, because the children were hungry, Stan wanted to stop off, and they went to one of those highway restaurants that straddle all six lanes. It was awful, awful and expensive. Anna grew tetchy, exasperated. She almost screamed that it was "disgusting, completely disgusting," and Lea, like something from a film by Godard, asked, "What does disgusting mean?" Anna walked out of the restaurant, leaving the children with Stan, and went to the car. She opened the back door, sat down among the toys, hid her head in her hands, and, quietly, started to sob.

LOUISE AND ALAIN

. . .

*T*HAT SAME SUMMER, it had not been quite so hot in Oslo. Romain had suggested Louise should go to Norway with him, while he attended an international colloquium: a wealthy foundation was bringing together the world's top language geneticists for three days.

"The high society of genetics will be there," Romain whispered to Louise.

He was so proud to be a part of it now.

They were put up at the Radisson Plaza, a luxury hotel close to the city center, where a welcome reception awaited them. The organizers had guessed that the colloquium would not be of much interest to partners: they handed out maps of Oslo, a history of the city, and a guide to its museums.

Romain introduced her to "John Vermont, Nobel Prize winner," pretending to forget that she knew him. Then Daniel Reynolds, "Nobel winner of tomorrow," and Janet Bilger and Tomomi Tsukuda, "Nobel winners of the day after tomorrow."

"You're the most beautiful," Romain whispered to Louise. She agreed.

As they were sitting down for dinner, Romain suggested to a delighted Vermont that he should sit beside her: the Nobel laureate was, as usual, smug and boring, and still had the same terrible bad breath. Louise left the table before dessert, claiming diplomatically to be tired from the trip. Romain took her hand for a moment, adding that he would join her later, and continued his conversation with Reynolds. She was not unhappy to get away. Romain was putting on his overzealous little boy act, and she loathed any dent in the respect she felt for him. The scene reminded her of one evening when they had argued after she watched, disappointed, as he tried like a bewitched child to get close to some obscure movie celebrity.

She changed and took the elevator all the way to the covered pool perched on the hotel roof. The bay windows looked down over Oslo's lights. The only person in the pool was swimming laps freestyle along one side. He did not pause when Louise dived in. After a few breaststrokes, she felt a bit cold and, with the first shiver, climbed out, settled on a lounge chair, and started reading the guide to Oslo. The swimmer's rhythm was slow and regular. At the end of the pool, he would exhale noisily and turn around underwater to start the next lap. Another ten minutes and he climbed up the ladder. He had shaved his head the way young balding men do, was probably past forty. His body was hairy, solid, not as muscular as his exercise led her to expect, and he was nearsighted too, because he groped for his glasses. He seemed surprised to see Louise, smiled at her and said a few words in Norwegian. She did not understand so he started again in English.

"Holidays?"

Louise smiled at his pronounced French accent. "Just for three days. And you?"

"I see . . . My English could do with some improvement. No, I work for Norsk Hydro." Louise shook her head and he explained: "Oil, aluminum, magnesium. I'm in aluminum. My name's Alain. Or Al. Like aluminum."

"Louise. Like Louise. Louise Blum."

She held out her hand. Alain was not French but Belgian, an engineer supervising the opening of a new manufacturing chain to the south of Oslo. He said a few words about what she should see: the natural history museum, its minerals collection, and the museum of Viking ships at Bygdøy. Then he apologized for leaving, he had to be up very early in the morning.

When Louise went to bed, Romain was still not back. Half a Noctimax helped her get to sleep.

The following morning, she declined the invitation to join the group of partners. She ventured into the city alone, with a few books in her bag, she explored the boutiques, bought herself a scarf. Following Alain's advice, she went and admired the long ships, then the gemstones and agates, before having elk meat for lunch on the wharf. She strolled through Vigeland Park and cruised along Oslo's fjord in a tourist boat. She returned to the hotel late in the evening, just in time for dinner, during which she was bored once again. She decided to go home to Paris. There was a flight in the morning, she would take it. Romain tried to dissuade her, but without really insisting. She was resolute: "Just say that Judith's ill, or Maud, that I was worried. I'm going to pack, I might go for a swim. Take your time, darling."

She went straight up to the pool. The Belgian engineer was doing his laps. Alain greeted her cheerfully and lay down on the lounge chair next to her. She told him about her day, the long ships and the smoked elk. There was a restful serenity about Alain, they talked for a long time, like old friends. He told her about his life without painting too grim a picture of it nor dressing it up. Recently divorced, a son of nearly twenty, a job that took too much of his time, a sick father—cancer. The separation from his wife had been violent, painful, he had started drinking but stopped in time. Alain was straightforward, strong, he was like his crawl, powerful and regular. His frank gaze lingered on Louise's legs, her stomach, her breasts. Louise did not dislike the fact that he liked her, even though she was not in the least attracted to him.

He was about to leave the pool, his face brightened: "Look, Louise, tomorrow morning I'm taking a couple of Norwegian friends to visit the factory in Holmestrand. Would you like to come with us and watch aluminum being melted in a furnace? It's impressive, really it is. We're leaving at nine-fifteen, it's only an hour away, and you'll be back by early afternoon, after lunch in the restaurant on the dam. It's very pure aluminum, the kind they use for the Airbus."

His enthusiasm was contagious. In the elevator, even though she did not find him attractive, she suddenly wanted this dumpy man to take her to his room, push her backward onto his bed, and undress her. She would have grasped his thick penis with her hand, her mouth, would probably have begged him to take her, crying out crude words as he drove deep into her. All things that were alien to her usual behavior, but miraculously authorized by the absence of love and the Norwegian night.

She went down to her floor, put herself to bed. She turned out the light and fondled herself in the dark to the point of pleasure. When Romain came in, she was asleep.

The following morning, she embarked on the Norwegian Air Oslo–Paris flight, an Airbus made of Alain's aluminum. She had left a note for him at reception, apologizing for her hasty departure: Maud was not well. At the end of August, Alain left a message at her office, having found the address: he was in Paris, he wanted to see her again. He called her again twice in early September. She never got back in touch.

STAN AND SIMON

. . .

"SO, DOCTOR, IS IT SERIOUS?"

Simon's voice bears the lighthearted imprint of a long-standing friendship. Anna's younger brother hopes he comes across to Stan as hard, impassive, but the way he rubs his thumb against his index finger betrays anxiety. Stan is scrutinizing the two angiographies on the screen: a dull, dark patch in the middle of the left retina leaves no room for doubt. The surgeon does not answer, enlarges the image, traces the scar line. He would like to find something reassuring to say. But nothing looks more like a Fuch's spot than another Fuch's spot.

Shit, Stan thinks, shit, Simon, how fucking stupid of you, how fucking stupid, you're always trying to be the best, the alpha male, always waiting till the last minute, you should have called me earlier, should have come immediately, this left retina's had it now, kaput, and microsurgery might have been a bit of a long shot, but I could have tried something, could have clawed back, I dunno, a couple of diopters for you, two diopters isn't so bad, it's better than blind, my poor brother, and what can I tell you about the right eye, because it's not looking good, nope, not looking good at all, having that first localized hemorrhage on the left retina, and let's have a closer look at the right retina, fuck, I can't believe it, you've got slight vascular weakness on that one too, there, right next to the optic nerve, it's a little bit too puffy, the bastard, you've got a one-in-four chance, let's be generous here, let's say one-in-eight that your other retina packs up in the next ten years, that gives us a one-in-three or -four chance you'll be blind by the time you're fifty, fuck, what do you want me to tell you, Simon, what do you want me to tell you, learn Braille, take up the piano again?

Stan sits down slowly on the corner of his desk, gives Anna's brother a wide smile: "Right . . . Simon . . . No need to panic. Look at this discolored area on your left retina: that's called a Fuch's spot. It's a pretty rare problem which occurs in the very nearsighted, like you or like me: I'm minus eight, you see, almost as bad. I'll explain: in nearsighted people the eye is too large so it exerts constant mechanical pressure on the retina, if this gets to be too much then a blood vessel can burst. That's what's happened. Because it was a large blood vessel—a small artery, you can see it here—the hemorrhage has damaged the macula, that's the part of the retina where the eye focuses."

"A busted artery," Simon says, adding sardonically, "alas, 'tis all in vein!"

Stan is still looking at the screen, does not hear the pun.

"It explains the gap in the middle of your field of vision. The good news is it won't spread, it's starting to cauterize. It never really spreads."

"Can it get better, heal up on its own?"

"It's healed, Simon. The eye has repaired itself. Well, as much as it can. It did it by scarring, and now the light-sensitive cells—you know, the rods and cones—that were starved of a blood supply have necrotized."

"But . . . Stan . . . Can you do laser treatment? Anna says you're the best surgeon in France, you work miracles, you have patients from all over the world, New York, Buenos Aires . . ."

"Oh, and why not Shanghai? Your sister really is unbeliev-able . . . Listen, it's true, you can treat it by injecting verte-porfin and then using lasers, but that only works in the first few hours, maybe the first few days. But this has been going on for at least three weeks, the scarring is permanent . . . Any-way, Simon, I wouldn't have risked laser treatment, the cure would have been worse than the complaint. Here, can you see that little fluorescent green zigzag? The vascular tear occurred two millimeters from the optic nerve. It's so close that I'd have risked touching it with the beam."

"What about retinal grafts? Can't you . . ."

"Stem cells? Listen, Simon, I don't like being pessimistic, but in my lab we follow new advances really closely: we won't be able to rely on that for another ten or twenty years. I'll be the first surgeon in France to know how to do it, I swear to you. What we can actually graft right now are retinal cells . . . in mice. But the stupid cells can't work out how to adapt them-selves to connect to the optic nerve. You could say it's like having a new retina but the brain has no idea it's there. You'll have to learn to live with this. You'll still have peripheral vi-sion in your left eye, and even though it will be tough at first, with your right eye correcting, you'll end up getting used to it. But Simon, the most important thing now is if you notice the slightest alteration in your field of vision, wavering, blind spots, changes in color, flashes of light, you don't fuck around, you don't wait two weeks before coming to see me, you call me and come to whichever hospital I'm at. And if I'm not around, because you never know, you ask for Herzog and say I sent you, he's very good. Actually, you know what? Go and see him. For a second opinion. I won't be upset, I can just imagine what you're going through right now."

"No, Stan, I won't disturb him, I have faith in you."

"No, I want you to: go and see Herzog. I really don't want you thinking I'm being all reassuring because you're my wife's brother and a friend."

"Thanks. I understand. But I won't go. And . . . isn't there some diet I can follow? Or food supplements? To nourish the retina? What about lusein? I've heard that—"

"Lutein. Avoid all those parapharmaceuticals . . . If you really want some lutein, you can get it from spinach, kiwi fruit, pretty much anything green . . . you can always fill your boots with that. For night vision, eat plenty of blueberries, like airline pilots. It works."

"Is there really no preventive treatment? Is there nothing I can do?"

"Nothing. Take a rain check on strenuous sport: soccer, squash, weight lifting, anything that rapidly increases pressure in the eye. Lose a bit of weight, do some cycling, some walking, that doesn't do anyone any harm. Anyway, you're only thirty-five, high blood pressure's not a problem."

Simon says nothing. He closes his right eye, looks in front of him, reaches out his arm and watches his hand disappear, swallowed up by the gray hole that the Fuch's spot has carved out in the middle of his vision. He leans his head back, takes a deep breath . . . Stan takes him by the shoulders.

"Simon . . . everything's fine."

"I've got this heavy weight crushing my chest, it's terrible, I can't breathe properly . . . If this happens to my right eye now, I won't be able to work anymore, or read, I won't be able to see Nadine's face, or the children's, I—"

"Don't worry, your right retina's absolutely fine. I know you're just as nearsighted on both sides, but it's pointless worrying. The risk of bilateralization—"

"The risk of what?"

"Of the same thing happening in the other eye . . . is very low."

"How low? I'm sorry to go on about this, Stan, but one in a hundred, in ten, in two?"

"I promise you, it's very rare, no one has reliable statistics. I have hundreds of patients with a Fuch's spot in one eye, and hardly any of them are affected in both."

Stan is lying. Sufficient unto the day . . .

"I'm going to give you a prescription. For some sedatives. I want you to take them, I haven't known a single patient who hasn't been depressed for a while. I'd expect it. Losing an eye is a shocking loss, these drugs are there to be used. I can even recommend a psychiatrist."

"No, come on." Simon is indignant.

Stan smiles and does not press the point. "Listen, Simon, I've just had an appointment canceled, let's have a closer look at the pressure in this right eye, because you're worried about it, and afterward we can have lunch in the hospital cafeteria. They may have some kiwis . . ."

Kiwis they have. Simon eats three of them.

That evening, Stan is on duty at Quinze-Vingts Hospital. Anna is worried, she calls him.

"Professional secret, my darling," Stan says, hoping he sounds casual. "It's like I thought, vascular damage. He's lost the central vision in his left eye."

"Permanently?"

"Yes. There's nothing I can try. But it'll be okay. Simon's very brave. I told him to go and see Herzog, but you know what your brother's like, he refused. Mind you, Herzog wouldn't have said or done anything more."

Anna does not reply. Stan keeps his most cheerful voice, wanting to dispel her sadness: "Are you still going out this evening, darling? Are you going to Christiane's?"

"Yes. My parents are here. They're going to keep an eye on the children at home."

"Are you going out on your own?"

"With Maureen. And another friend."

"Who's that?"

"Yves."

"Beaudouin? You're taking your manager to Christiane's party?"

"No. Yves Janvier. Someone Maureen knows. You don't know him. Bye."

"See you in the morning."

Anna hangs up.

She called Yves two days before, asking if he would like to join her for this party. Maureen served as an alibi, because Anna was not altogether lying: her cousin does know the writer, but hardly, having interviewed him a few years ago.

When Yves picked up the phone, she immediately forgot how to behave properly and her very first sentence burst out subconsciously: "Yves? On Friday, my husband's on duty . . ." Later, while they talked, Anna slipped in: "Maureen's single at the moment." She had a painful longing for him and Maureen to like each other so that Yves, having become Maureen's lover, would stop being a possibility. Yves did not grasp this. He suspected her of playing matchmaker.

Outside, Anna hears the dull clunk of the door to the elevator. She hopes it is Yves.

YVES AND ANNA

. . .

Y VES HAS NOT SEEN ANNA again since their first meeting. The elevator drops him off at her floor. There is only one door, and the hallway acts as storage space for children's bicycles, scooters, a little red Ferrari with pedals. So many warning signs: Anna's life is as cluttered as her hallway.

He rings the bell. A little boy opens the door—Karl, Yves remembers—and stares at him.

"Mommy, there's a man."

The child runs off.

"Come in, Yves," Anna's voice calls out. "Did you say hello, Karl?"

Yves takes one step into the foyer, Anna is still invisible. Her voice comes to him along the corridor, from her bedroom, Yves presumes.

"I'm sorry, I'm not dressed yet. My parents will keep you company."

Yves takes another step. It is a nice apartment with a mish-mash of furniture, strongly biased toward the sixties. A woman wearing a lot of gold and pearls and with a Sephardic beauty is sitting in an armchair smoothing a little girl's blond curls for the night. Yves recognizes Anna's smile in hers.

"Hello . . . I'm Anna's mother. Beatrice. You know her, al-ways late. Well, aren't you going to say hello, Lea?"

Lea, sulking, does not look up. Her grandmother does not push her.

"Laurent, my husband."

Yves has not noticed the man with the long white hair and regal features standing by the bookshelves, leafing through a book.

"Good evening. Laurent Stein, the father of the woman who's late."

Yves shakes his hand: "Yves Janvier."

"I know," says Laurent Stein, turning over the book's cover. Yves recognizes *The Two-Leaf Clover*. "It's my reading for this evening," Anna's father explains. "It starts really well."

"Thanks. But it ends badly. Luckily it's very short."

"It ends badly, it's very short . . . That's a definition of life." Yves smiles. Anna's father watches him, half opens the book. "Do you mind if I make a criticism? Or let's call it just a comment."

"Please do."

"It's about the quote from Pascal that you use as an epigraph: 'We never love a person, but only qualities.'"

"Yes?"

"I'm sorry, but I wonder whether it's not the exact op-posite: what attracts us about another person has more to do with what makes them fragile, the chink in their armor.

Love is kindled by the weakness we perceive, the flaw we get in through, wouldn't you say?"

Yves is disoriented, wants to argue the point. "Perhaps. But I felt Pascal used the word 'qualities' to mean character traits in general . . ."

"I'm afraid his meaning was more prosaic. I have to admit I loathe Pascal. He's a narrow-minded, third-rate philosopher pinioned by superstition. To be honest, I can't think of anything more stupid than his challenge."[3]

"I'm with you on that," Yves smiles.

Anna interrupts, her voice amused: "I'll be quick, Yves, or my father will corner you and then we'll be really late. And you, daddy, stop teasing Yves. Yves, if my father's bothering you—"

"Not in the least, your father's not bothering me . . ."

"Are you working on a novel at the moment, Mr. Janvier?"

"Yves. Please, Mr. Stein, call me Yves . . . Yes, I've started on something, about a relationship . . . Well, when I put it like that, it sounds terribly banal . . ."

"No it doesn't. Do you have a title yet?"

"I'd like to call it *The Together Theory,* together as in 'being together,' not 'get it together.' Or maybe *Abkhazian Dominoes,* I'm not sure yet."

"Abkhazian?"

"From Abkhazia. It's a small state to the north of the Black Sea."

3. Pascal published a challenge, offering prizes for solutions to two complex mathematical problems involving Cavalieri's calculus of indivisibles, problems he himself had already solved. He sent the challenge out to Wren, Laloubère, Leibniz, Huygens, Wallis, Fermat, and several other mathematicians.

"They're both good titles. A bit intellectual, though, wouldn't you say? My daughter's right, I'm teasing you."

"Um . . . Yes, what I wanted was—"

"Okay, I'm ready."

Anna emerges from the bedroom, sheathed in a red satin dress with oriental patterns on it. Yves thinks she looks dazzling. She has bare feet, and is holding a pair of sandals in each hand.

"Mom, do you think these ones, the Cretan look, or these which are more Roman?"

Yves can see no difference at all. The mother can, though. She opts for the Cretan pair.

"We're off, mom. Maureen's just called. She can't find anywhere to park and she's waiting outside. Bye, daddy. Kids, are you going to give me a kiss?"

Lea and Karl hurtle out of their room and almost suffocate her with hugs, Lea acting abandoned, laughing as she pretends to snivel. Anna tears herself away from them gently in the hallway. She goes into the elevator and Yves follows her. He has one last look at the little red Ferrari. The door closes.

There are four inches separating Yves and Anna. She wears a fresh perfume, all woods and ivy, she says nothing, smiles, lowers her eyes. To resist the urge to take her in his arms, Yves concentrates on their surroundings: elevator branded ART, tinted mirror, coarse black carpeting on the walls. A copper plaque: MAX: 3 PEOPLE, 240 KG. A control panel with six black buttons, GROUND, 1, 2, 3, 4, 5, one red button, STOP, one green button, 24 HR. CALL. A cutout area covered with wire netting, a loudspeaker, and a microphone. IN THE EVENT OF AN INCIDENT, PLEASE REFER TO TL1034.

But there is no incident, and the trip down takes fifteen seconds. Yves succeeds in trying nothing. All through the evening he will not have another opportunity, however slight, to kiss Anna. She and her cousin Maureen will go home early.

In the morning, when Stan comes home from night duty, she will tell him about Christiane's party, at length, more than usual. About Jean, Maureen's new boyfriend, "charming, but maybe a bit smug," about Christiane's illness, "stabilized," about the famous and very talented filmmaker who was there, "of course you remember, Stan, *Thirty Years Without Seeing the Sea*, he directed that, we saw it together."

"*Thirty Years Without Seeing the Sea*," Stan says. "Yes."

About Yves, Anna says nothing.

ROMAIN AND LOUISE

• • •

Paris, October 3, midnight.

Romain, it's late, you're still working at the lab and I'm writing this letter on the computer while I wait for you, which is ~~in fact~~ my way of not waiting for you. It's nighttime, I've put ~~the~~ our children to bed, they're asleep. ~~I haven't written to you for a long time~~ I wish I didn't have to write you this letter. Maybe I'm only writing it so that I've written it, and ~~I'm hesitating~~ I don't know if I'll give it to you. When you leave a man, what's the point of explaining?

I've met a man, Romain ~~I made lo~~. I think what matters isn't the person, but the fact that I could, that I wanted to meet him. I was surprised, surprised to feel so little guilt, so little shame. Just happy like a ~~girl~~ kid ~~of twenty of fifteen~~ on her first date.

We've been together ten years, Romain. I have so much affection for you. Over the years, you've become my best friend, almost a brother. But, of course, you can't be a brother. That ~~wouldn't~~ doesn't mean anything anymore. Sometimes, at night, I lie next to you, I touch your skin, I want some intimacy, sometimes sex, without really wanting you. I'm forty years old, or will be in a few months. It's not the first time ~~I've been unfaithful~~ I've wanted ~~a man~~ another man. ~~In fact~~ It's the first time that there's been nothing there to stop me, that I can't picture for a minute not seeing him again.

~~Romain, I'd like I want we need~~

Louise closes the document without saving it, switches off the computer. She will never find the words to describe the abandon Thomas has brought about in her; it is crucial that she does not find them. She would like to venture an image—a window thrown open by a squall, sugar melting in coffee—but this is about bodies, nudity, desire, a stark, self-evident need, and she had no say in the matter. Yes, that's it, she thinks. I didn't have any say in it. Louise smiles to think how Thomas would interpret her choice of expression.

She is in love, she craves sugar, eats a dried apricot, another. All at once she is really tired. She will not wait any longer for Romain, and goes to bed. She is not guilty because, she keeps telling herself, thrilled, she had no say in it. She falls asleep immediately.

THOMAS AND LOUISE

. . .

I T IS LATE. The Thursday evening patient has left. Thomas looks at his *Le Monde*, rereads the date bitterly. Tomorrow it will be twenty-six years since Piette died. The photo Thomas always keeps on his desk shows her smiling, lying on a bed with pages of notes scattered around her. She is four months pregnant. She will lose the baby in a few weeks' time, and commit suicide a year later. On the back of the snapshot, Thomas has written out a canzone from *La vita nuova*, the blue ink is gradually fading:

Sì che volendo far come coloro	*So that I desire to be like one*
Che per vergogna celan lor mancanza,	*Who, to conceal his poverty through shame,*
Di fuor mostro allegranza,	*Shows joy outwardly,*
E dentro da lo core struggo e ploro.	*And within my heart am troubled and weep.*

There are some works so luminous that they fill us with shame for the meager life to which we are resigned, that they implore us to lead another, wiser, fuller life; works so powerful that they give us strength, and force us to new undertakings. A book can play this role. For Thomas, it is *La vita nuova*, in which Dante weeps for his Beatrice. A friend gave it to him shortly after Piette's death. But Thomas does not believe that his Piette waits for him in a future life, he doubts that anywhere in the infinite plurality of Lewis's worlds there is a peaceful universe where a happy Piette gave birth to their little boy.

There are two other photographs on the desk: the larger frame holds a picture of his daughters, Alice and Esther, they are five and seven years old, sitting astride ponies, with their mother. The divorce is already under way. The third picture, black-and-white, shows three men, two of them are recognizably Lacan and Barthes. The youngest, in the middle, has the thick black hair of a twenty-year-old, he is smiling, holding a bulging file in his hand. Thomas is now the least identifiable. Piette took it at the Collège de France, in January 1978. It gives the impression that they are the best of friends, Lacan seems to be laughing at a joke the young psychology student has made. If anyone is sufficiently inquisitive to ask about it, he just says, "That's me with Jacques and Roland."

From his office, Thomas has heard the door to the gate opening, recognized the metallic click of Louise's heels on the paving stones in the courtyard and the staircase, and has opened the door before she could knock. He does not really like displaying how eager he is to see her every time, but he is even less keen to affect patience.

She sees him on the landing and smiles. "What if it wasn't me?"

"I don't know anyone who walks like you."

"I'll sound different when I'm carrying a suitcase."

"Which means?"

"Soon, as soon as I can find the courage, I'm going to talk to Romain. I'll tell him I want us to separate. I'll tell him about you too. Something inside me's broken and it won't come back together again. And it's not just since we met. Do you still want anything to do with me, this madwoman with two children?"

"Yes."

"Because you do realize I'm mad, don't you?"

Thomas looks at Louise, smiles. "I'm very happy to have a madwoman. I've always wanted to take work home with me."

ANNA AND YVES

· · ·

ANNA HAS NOT SEEN YVES again since Christiane's party. He sent her a recent piece of writing, a play for four characters, and they have arranged to meet in a bistro on the rue de Belleville.

When Anna arrives, she looks around the room, sees him, and is amazed not to have recognized him. She thought he was taller, a ridiculous idea given he is sitting down, remembers a younger man, had not noticed how much hair had deserted his forehead. He is reading a magazine, has a cup of coffee, catches sight of her, smiles. The thrill that has gripped her every other time fails to materialize. She was as apprehensive about the sensation as she was looking forward to it, and the fact that she does not feel it frustrates and placates her at the same time.

She sits down and launches straight into criticizing the dialogue, the trajectory of the play, confessing that she prefers novels. He offers to show her his first novel: he lives very close by, the coffee is much better at his apartment, she accepts. Walking beside him, the feeling grips her again, just as acute, and she welcomes it excitedly.

They cut across the tree-lined courtyard of a renovated apartment building, climb the stairs, and he opens the door to a spacious apartment with high ceilings and a warm masculine atmosphere. The huge, bright living room is littered with a jumble of things, movie lighting equipment, an *écorché* model in an opera hat, a driftwood sculpture. Anna walks over to the large bay window, looks at Paris gradually picked out by sunlight, the basilica of Sacré Coeur, Beaubourg to the south, the apex of the Eiffel Tower in the distance. Yves rummages through a cardboard box, takes out a book, and hands it to Anna.

"I've found it. There you are. Sorry about the mess, Anna. I've only just moved in."

"It's huge."

"Yes. Too big for me and my daughter."

"Do you rent it?"

"No, I have too many different employers to keep a landlord happy. I've always had to buy. I live off my capital."

So it is possible then, Anna thinks, quashed. She had pictured a dirty, dilapidated building, a small cluttered apartment, modest means, even slight embarrassment. She wanted him to be poor, wanted his poverty to make him unthinkable, she would have preferred having some excuse at hand, wanted to be able to say reproachfully: "Whatever sort of life could you offer my children?"

"I promised you a coffee. Over here."

Anna cannot help smiling at the American-style kitchen: she and Stan have the same design, from the same Swedish supplier.

She walks ahead of him, he breathes in her perfume. She moves very slowly. Yves will learn later that when she cannot cope with tension, she slows her pace as if the moment itself were taking all her energy. Now she stops altogether, suffocating. Yves's arms are around her, she does not push him away, his arms turn her, she pivots, Yves draws her to him, she half opens her lips, he takes them. Without a word, he leads her to the bedroom, she lets herself be led.

ANNA AND STAN

· · ·

*T*HE DAY AFTER, an earthquake comes on an evening like any other. The children are in their bedroom, Lea drawing, Karl practicing his scales on the piano. Anna is preparing dinner and Stan is setting the table. Anna talks about her day: a young autistic patient said the word "chocolate" for the first time.

Stan does not ask many questions, listens to his wife, watches her affectionately. Talking is never an effort for Anna. The more tired she is the more she seems to ramble.

While she cooks, Anna has put her rings on the counter. They are all presents from Stan. Her narrow wedding band punctuated by thirty-three diamonds. A chunkier ring, an ancient-looking disk of yellow gold set with uncut rubies and sapphires and mounted on a band of white gold; she has never known what it cost, it was an unreasonable amount. Finally, a simple red-and-black agate pearl, mounted on a circle of silver, she chose it at a market in Avignon, when she and Stan still used to go to the theater festival, before the children were born.

Anna cuts up fennel, turnips, and zucchini, tosses them into a frying pan, sprinkles mild spices, and covers them with a glass lid that immediately steams up. The rice is boiling in a saucepan. A sad expression, tinted with irritation, hovers over her face. She feels as if, rather than wanting to be somewhere else, she already is somewhere else. Looking at her own life through a window.

She drains the rice and puts her rings back onto her wet fingers. She suddenly grasps the fact that if she leaves Stan, if he becomes involved with another woman, she would feel no jealousy at all. She knows everything about the life the woman would lead, Stan's thoughtfulness, his least little consideration, she even knows what presents he would give her, would have no trouble recognizing them on the new girlfriend's fingers, around her neck.

She puts the steaming rice into a bowl, also thinking of all the women Yves has known, women about whom she knows nothing. She pictures them happy, walking arm in arm, cleaving to him. These are fleeting images, but so violently sensual that they disturb her.

"What are you thinking about?" asks Stan.

"I'm so sorry," Anna replies, spontaneously.

It is not an answer, it is an admission. If Stan realizes this, he does not show it, goes on pouring water into the children's glasses.

"Are you thinking about your brother's Fuch's spot?"

Anna does not reply.

"It's a really rare condition, you know. It could easily not happen to the other eye. He'll just have to be vigilant, that's all."

"Karl, Lea, it's ready."

She has pulled herself together, her voice is cheerful.

LOUISE AND THOMAS

• • •

THOMAS HAS HAD A NIGHTMARE and is describing it to Louise in a quiet café on the Place de la Contrescarpe: "I'm in my kitchen with Maud—"

"What, my Maud? My daughter?" Louise interjects.

"Yes. You've shown me a picture of her, but I wouldn't recognize her in the street. In my dream, she looks a bit like Judy Garland in *The Wizard of Oz*, in other words nothing like herself. I'm teaching her to make pancakes. There's a bulky old TV in the kitchen with a film on. It's a spy film, a black-and-white B movie. A woman's been tied up in a kitchen exactly like mine. A man comes in from time to time and slaps her. She wants to scream but she's gagged. I know that the woman is you, even though she doesn't look at all like you, and I also know that although the scene is innocuous, Maud finds it terrifying. But it doesn't occur to me to switch the TV off, I just try to get between her and the screen, and I talk very loudly to drown out the woman's moans. A man in a suit, who could be Humphrey Bogart in *Casablanca*, comes in and yells at the woman, 'Go home, now.' She's immediately released and limps away, turning around to throw him a pack of Q-tips."

"A pack of what?"

"I know, it's ridiculous, it was a dream, I can't think what the Q-tips are meant to be. The TV stops all by itself, I hope Maud didn't see any of it, and I yammer on about yeast making the pancake batter rise. Your little girl looks at me angrily, she wanted to watch the film."

"Is that it?" Louise says.

"That's it. I'm telling you because I think it has to do with my guilt."

"Is Humphrey Bogart my husband? Wasn't Bogart really short?" she laughs, shaking her head.

"I don't know if it's him. Dreams are always complex."

"I don't have nightmares, I just have an impossible client. A rapist. He's chosen a completely untenable line of defense. I said: 'Look, stop this, don't be so stupid, she has bruises where she was hit, and the fluid found on her clothes is your sperm.'"

Hearing the word "sperm" pronounced too loudly, the whole café turns toward them and falls silent, but Louise does not notice. She continues: "Just admit that you raped this girl. The jury's never going to believe you. If you carry on denying it, you won't be getting four or five years, but ten."

"Louise . . ."

"Yes?"

"Don't talk so loud. Everyone's looking at us. Well, it's me they're all looking at."

Louise turns around. All eyes are on Thomas, brimming with anger and contempt. She stands up immediately and addresses them all.

"Let's stop right there. I'm a lawyer. This is the love of my life and I'm telling him about my day at work, I love him, we're getting married on Sunday."

She sits down beside Thomas and kisses him full on the mouth. The kiss lasts some time, there is whistling, some laughter, clapping even. When she breaks away from him, Thomas roars with laughter.

"You really are crazy."

"About you."

ANNA AND YVES

· · ·

ESIRE WILL NOT ALLOW for simple explanations. When a cat runs after a mouse, it is not because cat molecules are drawn to mouse molecules. Anna does not understand why her body likes Yves's hands so much, no more than Yves can explain what drives his hands toward Anna's body.

Because she allows him to do everything, everything feels natural. Nothing is shameless anymore. Or is it because nothing goes against nature that there is nothing she forbids him? All the same, one evening, after he has taken her way beyond the bounds of convention, she is suddenly worried and whispers: "If you write a book about us one day, don't talk about that."

"What do you mean 'that'?" Yves asks.

"You know what I mean. That."

Yves shakes his head, kisses her. Why worry, he could never put it into words.

Anna does not like Yves's desire to be derived from her own. She would sometimes like his passion not to be addressed to her, would like him to take her "as a woman," "just like that," so she is reduced to an object in his hands, losing herself in an almost mechanical thirst for sex. She once had a lover—"a bit of a prick," she admits—who, seeing her naked, said, "A woman is such a beautiful thing," and that sentence struck her as the most wonderful declaration. Yves, by contrast, finds it utterly predictable, naive, the pronouncement of a truck-driver poet, of a romantic in a wifebeater.

"I don't give a damn," she retorts, "I like it. It sets me free."

Yet when they make love, Yves speaks her name, and the crude and gentle things he says make her head spin: "I love it when you call me Anna. It's disturbing, like it's new to me."

Several times, she asks for a touch of violence. She says: Bite me, hit me. Yves, amused, does as he is asked, finds he knows how to, joins in the game. He quickly reaches his boundaries. He is happy to play along, but with too much pretending, he loses track of himself and of his desire.

After their pleasure, when their bodies refuse to cooperate anymore, the appetite they have for each other is still just as sharp. Anna kisses his neck, Yves fondles her breasts, the back of her neck, her buttocks, amazed by this hunger he cannot satisfy.

"My breasts are getting old," she grumbles. "You've never known them any different, but they were so much better before. Arrogant, that's the word. They were arrogant."

He licks her nipples and they harden beneath his tongue, he nibbles them, takes them in his mouth. They are no longer a young girl's breasts, and that moves him, deeply. Sometimes, appeased, Anna falls asleep, and the soft outline of a smile stays on her lips.

Another time, as she is putting her clothes back on, Yves pushes her down onto the bed again, unceremoniously spreads her thighs and plants a kiss on her pussy. Anna lets him manhandle her, laughing. When Yves stands up, she asks wistfully: "Why can't I be like I am with you when I'm with Stan?"

She is sincere in her regret, painfully so. It is true, everything would be so much easier. Yves smiles. He has a remarkable capacity for taking these blows on the chin.

Like a teenager, Anna also frequently asks him: "Why do you love me, Yves, why do you love me so much?"

She is not simpering. She wishes the love he felt for her could give her some parameters, convince her she exists, because she exists so fully for him. She would like to feel consistent, as dense and heavy as a clay golem that never questions itself like this. She has such a need for other people. She sometimes says she is just a saprophytic plant, a parasite with a gift for life.

When Anna finally leaves, Yves likes staying in his apartment, making the most of the powerful inertia created by the happiness he feels when he is with her. If he has accepted an invitation for a drink or dinner, he cancels it, claiming he is busy, has a migraine. He wants nothing and no one to obliterate the note he can still hear inside, to disturb the color she has set down in him.

ANNA AND LOUISE

. . .

TWO HUNDRED EUROS for a wool sweater, nearly a hundred for a simple black cotton scarf. Yves has hardly ever set foot in such an expensive boutique. Before Anna erupted into his life, he had no dealings with these almost empty places, half art gallery, half salon, where not one dress, not one skirt, not one coat on the racks is a duplicate, where there is often only one size—but one that seems to fit almost all the customers. All the clothes have the supreme elegance to appear not completely new.

"No, it's not expensive, look, they're half price," Anna corrects him, "it's a sale."

Clothes are a compulsive passion of Anna's. She follows fashion closely, knows how to work it, mix trends. Beside her, Yves slightly tarnishes the picture, with his walking shoes and his old duffel coat. She would like to dress him from head to foot, make him "sharp," elegant. She already influences him: he sometimes wears fine shoes, dark shirts, pants with front pleats. Watching Anna in a boutique, her unselfconscious display of narcissism, amuses Yves far more than it annoys him. He senses that she wants to know just how far he will tolerate this addiction, this fondness for what she calls "an aesthetic" and which she has no intention of losing.

Anna likes being attractive, and does not want to give that up now or later, when age catches up with her. She admires those women who fight every step of the way, and still want to resist the injustices of time in their sixties. She sees nothing ridiculous about wanting to appear twenty years old right to the end. She is vigilant. One lunchtime, when Anna is walking arm in arm with Yves on the rue Oberkampf, they bump into a girlfriend of hers. The woman is still young, very slim, athletic-looking. A sudden ray of sunlight is cruel to her: in its glare, from that angle, the woman's white skin looks like fragile ancient parchment. Anna shudders. They have barely said goodbye to the woman before Anna rushes into a pharmacy to buy some hydrating cream.

Another day, because she does not have enough time to go up to his apartment and she "doesn't want to make love in five minutes," he joins her downstairs, in her car. She suggests they just go for a drink in the café across the street. She takes out her bright red lipstick, eases it onto her lower lip, closes her mouth to spread it, then assesses the result in the rearview mirror. Now enhanced, she looks at him.

"Do you want me to do my eye makeup as well?"

He thinks she looks perfect.

"The actress Romy Schneider always put on makeup when her husband suggested they go out," she adds, "even just for lunch in the restaurant downstairs."

Mirrors are important. There are three of them in Yves's apartment: the big one above the fireplace in the living room, the small one in the bathroom, over the sink, and the last one, a tall full-length mirror, in the bedroom, on the door of a closet. When Anna has to go home, each of them plays its part. First, in the bathroom, she checks the small details, then looks at the bigger picture in the bedroom, and finally proceeds to a general inspection in the living room.

He wonders whether this preoccupation with appearance could come between them one day. Anna's father is right, though: you fall in love with the flaw. Yves knows this. In his apartment he has a wall light that he commissioned from a sculptor friend, and when it first arrived he was disappointed. He did not dislike it, but it was not what he expected. Now, though, that is partly what he likes about this wall light. It never quite manages to disappear, it is a palpable presence. He does not want a woman who blends in with the background either. Besides, Anna is many things, but not a wall light.

Anna cannot make up her mind between two dresses, one in pink and green, short, very 1960s Courrèges, and a longer, more sensible one in gray and red. The pretty blond woman beside her is facing the same dilemma.

"It really is very pretty," says Anna, who has tried on the shorter one, "but I can't wear it for work, and I'd never dare go out in it."

"Well, I'll buy it then," says Louise, laughing, "I'll wear it at the law courts under my long black robes."

ANNA AND YVES

. . .

SOME NIGHTS when Stan is on duty at the Quinze-Vingts, Yves drops in to see Anna on the rue Érasme, after she has put the children to bed. She cooks dinner for two and spends the evening in his arms, always worried Karl might wake and catch them together.

One evening, Anna takes Yves to her bedroom. She opens a closet, eases out three dusty shoe boxes, and carries them to the kitchen. In them are hundreds of photographs. She lays out her life before Yves, perhaps for him. It is a long time since she has looked inside these boxes.

He recognizes her in the dark-haired little girl in overalls using every inch of her body to thrust a swing into the blue of the sky; in the girl on the brink of adolescence dancing with her father, almost like a woman in love. In another she is wearing a white dress, sitting in a boat on a pond in a landscaped garden. The picture could have been taken in the 1920s. Yves recognizes the man holding the oars. He is a writer. "Isn't that Hugues Léger with you, in that boat?"

"It is. Do you know him?"

"Not very well. I really like his books, we used to have the same publisher."

"He and I were together, for a year. We're still friends. I could get you together for dinner if you like."

She continues rummaging through the boxes, takes out photographs of her wedding, pointing things out, making comments. Yves thinks that, in front of him, with him, Anna is drawing up the inventory of everything she is preparing to lose. Right now, she is asking him to find the words that will help her draw on her own strength to give up what each photo says. Look at this happiness, my happiness, my husband, my house, my children, my parents, look. It's all there, spread out on this kitchen table, years of life in fading colors, I give them to you, I'll abandon them for you, my love. But what about you, what are you offering? Tell me that.

Anna is afraid she will never "be able to do it." Sometimes, in order to convince herself, she cites Jane Birkin, Romy Schneider, other women—often actresses—who had several significant men in their lives; what Anna actually says is "several lives," as if each man counted as a life. She looks for role models, examples, who say, Yes, she has a right to this too. Because it is something she is owed.

But she has her doubts.

"You know," she says one evening when they are in the car, "I worry so much about not being able to do it. I often just tell myself: Anna, don't. Do it."

Yves bursts out laughing. "Did you hear what you just said? You said, 'Don't do it.'"

Anna did hear herself. All her ambivalence is in those words. "Don't. Do it" or "Don't do it." All down to a period and the subconscious.

HUGUES AND YVES

. . .

I DON'T KNOW if I have a best friend. Sometimes I can wake up and not know how old I am. I've set my clock ten minutes fast to make sure I leave on time, but I now take the extra ten minutes into account, which cancels them out. I'd like to write a book with the title *A Book Not Worth Reading* and have it published by a company called Minor Press in a collection known as Complete Obscurity, so that I can say: "I had a book not worth reading published in complete obscurity by a minor press." I was once left by a woman, and I cut my mattress in two, so that I didn't have to sleep on her side. I can never find my keys when I have to go out in a hurry. I like the pillow to be cool when I go to bed. I once knew a man called Deadman who introduced himself like this: "Deadman, like dead man without the gap." I will go to hell. I've watched the image of the tsunami unleashing itself onto the Indonesian coast at least ten times on television. I own sneakers, tennis shoes, climbing boots (worn only twice), lace-up walking boots, black moccasins, elegant black shoes, slippers, rubber-soled sandals, and yellow flippers. I know that my favorite film isn't a very good film. I often wonder what would be different about the world if I didn't exist.

Yves puts down Hugues Léger's first book, *Definition*. A litany of sentences, almost a thousand of them, in which the writer sketches a self-portrait in disjointed fragments. The previous evening, Hugues killed himself, at home, with a bullet through the mouth. Anna is in Berlin for a few days, she probably does not yet know. Yves immediately wrote an obituary for *Libération*, and managed to arrange through a journalist friend for it to be published, even though a different article had already been approved for the page layout. In it he said this did not mean that Hugues's last book, *Autolyze*, which deals with suicide, should be seen as "a will waiting to be unsealed"; it was not "the cathartic book his friends would have liked to see him write, the book that would open up the creative field he still needed to open. But *Autolyze*, his most accomplished book, could exist in its own right without the dim reflected light of his death, which he need not have foretold."

The dinner Anna wanted would never happen, today's lover would never meet yesterday's. But Yves feels a blossoming friendliness toward Hugues, whose resolute death tries in vain to forbid friendship. He has reread his books, hoping to find in them the man Anna must have loved, and has identified a dark intelligence of life in his sentences. One he found particularly touching, violently so, was the closing sentence of *Definition*: "The best day of my life may already be behind me." Before meeting Anna, Yves also thought the best day of his life was already behind him. He also knows that the woman who caused Hugues to cut his mattress in two is Anna. She is the sort of woman you might want to sacrifice a bed for.

Anna harbored more than affection for Hugues.

"You know, Hugues," she once reassured him, "if you're ever having difficulties, you can always come and stay with us for a few days. It wouldn't be a problem, we have a guest room."

One evening—two years later—he rang their doorbell, suitcase in hand. He had had a row with his partner, he was out on the street. Anna was in Normandy and Stan opened the door. He did not know what to say to the man in the hallway: he did not know him, Anna had never mentioned any invitation and, since then, Karl had been born and the guest room was now his. Stan asked Hugues in before calling Anna. She explained the new situation to her old boyfriend. Hugues did not take offense but went and slept in a hotel, in spite of Stan's offer to put a cot in his office.

When she told Yves this anecdote, there was nostalgia in her voice. She had grown apart from Hugues, she said with regret, it would have been an opportunity to know each other in a different way, to become proper friends. But she actually said this: "It's a shame. If Hugues had stayed with us, we could have had a different relationship."

Yves laughed at the ambiguity. He knows that when Anna talks about "having a relationship," it almost always means a sexual one.

ANNA AND THOMAS

. . .

ANNA HAS NEVER KEPT COUNT of her sessions with Le Gall, but Le Gall writes the number 1,000 at the top of the page. That's a lot. You could have bought yourself a nice Porsche with some optional extras, Yves calculated. He is wrong: Thomas has paid off a small house in an Italian village near La Spezia.

Anna knows what she wants to talk about, Simon's eyesight problem. The thought that her brother could one day go blind terrifies her. She talks about Simon's wife, his children. Eventually, she confesses the fear she would feel if the man she loved could no longer capture her with his gaze, if she disappeared from his view, if that mirror she so needs were broken. The selfishness of this narcissism fills her with shame.

She also wants to talk about a Freudian slip she made the day before. She was out for a walk with Karl and Lea, and Yves was with them, they were all going out for lunch together for the first time. When she is with her children, Yves is never a lover, but a "friend." Anna has not yet resolved to admit the position he holds in her life, Yves often doubts she ever will. She refrains from any affectionate gestures, any attentiveness. Karl ran on ahead, jumping from one paving stone to another, Lea slipped between the two of them, took one of their hands each and started to swing, screeching happily. The spontaneous affection Lea always shows for Yves unsettles Anna every time: her daughter could be consenting to this unavowed, unacknowledged union, granting her mother's lover a role. Lea suddenly abandoned them to go look in a toy store window.

"We're late and we're hungry," Anna scolded her. "Come on, Nora, hurry up!" Nora? Anna looked away, disconcerted, then pulled herself together: "Quickly, Léa!"

Nora. She cannot get over it. She called her daughter by her younger sister's name, she was back in her childhood, in the days when she went for walks with her father, her mother, her sister, and her brothers. Lea did not appear to notice and hurried up.

Anna thought about this slip of the tongue all evening. She found an explanation, has already given it to Yves, and now produces it for Le Gall.

"I just can't be a mother when I'm with Yves."

"Mmm. But it wasn't Yves you were talking to."

"No."

"It was to Lea, wasn't it?"

"Yes."

"So," he suggests, "it could also be that in front of Lea and Karl, you can't be a woman. You won't let yourself."

Anna stays silent. Le Gall has just inverted her view of the scene, giving the slip the exact opposite meaning. She feels he has pinpointed it.

"Maybe I'm trying to protect them."

"Or to protect yourself."

Le Gall rarely intervenes. He does it every time he sees another plausible and equally productive association. He tries to banish the word "because" from his vocabulary. It is not up to him to determine what is cause and what is effect. He limits himself merely to stating facts. Sometimes, all he does is reiterate what has been said. During one session, she blurted, "If I stay with Yves, I'll have the life I'm dreaming of."

Thomas repeated this: "Yes. The life you're dreaming of. You're dreaming."

"Stan made me a mother," she told Le Gall, "Yves made me a woman."

Le Gall calls this formulization: a technique for turning life into aphorisms, for fixing it in words. It has its uses. Anna so likes "finding the words." But does finding the words mean understanding? Animals do not need words. Thomas Le Gall sometimes has his doubts about the philosophy of language, but having doubts about philosophy—whether or not it has to do with language—surely that in itself is truly philosophy?

STAN AND YVES

. . .

CORPORATE SPONSORSHIP improves a company's image, and the cost is tax-deductible. These two reasons explain why a water treatment corporation has raised the Pension Heisberg (what was once a private house, in the Marais district of Paris) to the ranks of a cultural venue. It finances concerts, discussions, and exhibitions there. On this particular evening, the Heisberg's auditorium is playing host to three writers for a joint reading, on the politically correct theme of Foreignness. Their three original texts were specially commissioned and have been published as a limited edition by Carnets Heisberg, printed in twelve-point type on laid paper.

Stan is late, he had an emergency keratitis. He has not been to a reading for a long time, but the children are with their grandparents for the night, Anna has gone to the rue de Verneuil for her psychoanalysis seminar, and curiosity got the better of him. He locked his bike close to the Picasso Museum and ran all the way to the Heisberg. The young blonde in glasses sitting at the small book table replies almost in a whisper: "Yes, sir, it's started. Yes, there are a few seats left. No, Yves Janvier hasn't done his reading yet, he's the last. You can slip in quietly through the upstairs door."

The audience is applauding. Stan opens the door and sits down quickly, right at the back of the auditorium. There is a man standing onstage, it is Janvier, he reads:

1. Hello. This text is called Foreign News, although the concept of news may be completely foreign to it. 2. Foreign News comprises seventy-eight entries, which is a reasonable and well-reasoned number, and is written to respect the constraint that every sentence will include the word foreign or foreigner. 3. In some cases the word could refer to a female foreigner. 4. It could also be in the plural, in which case it will be "foreigners" with an *s*. 5. Anyone who fails to put an *s* at the end of a plural word has a good chance of being one of these foreigners. 6. We will, therefore, see "foreign" the adjective and "foreigner" the noun, but there is absolutely no related verb. 7. If there were a verb "to foreign," it would be conjugated thus: I foreign, you foreign, he foreigns, etc. 8. What could you foreign? I have no idea. 9. Besides, why should the verb be transitive?

so this is the guy then, this is the guy, anna, you said "I found him unsettling," you even said "more than I've ever found any other man, well, since you, since we met, our marriage, I found him unsettling," but just look at him, anna, he's not that great, this yves janvier, not that young, anna, and balding, he's tall, yes, true but no more than I am, and older too, with wrinkles and bags under his eyes, a bit of a gut maybe even, I can't see properly, greasy hair, his forehead's shining, anyway, he's not at all your type, anna, it's weird, the more I look at him the more I think he's just not your type, a

But to foreign oneself sounds embarrassingly like to fondle oneself. 10. In Exodus (23:9) it says: "Also thou shalt not oppress a foreigner: for ye know the heart of a foreigner, seeing ye were foreigners in the land of Egypt." 11. One last quote: "I am man, and nothing human is foreign to me." This is from Terence (185–159 BC); I copied it out into a little yellow notebook when I was thirteen years old. 12. The thirteen-year-old boy I was then would probably listen to what I am saying now and think I was speaking a foreign language. 13. I'm sure he would be terrified if you told him that in thirty-seven years' time he would be the one speaking that foreign language. 14. Perhaps I would

good voice, he has a good voice and some presence, I'll give you that, I'm going to listen to what he's saying, concentrate, it's only twenty minutes, after all, twenty minutes to understand, no, you really can't find this guy attractive, I can't see anything about him, and then there's this ridiculous piece which never gets going, doesn't have anything to say, it's just there, how complacent, how pretentious, the audience is listening, though, what kind of constraint is that as a writer, just integrating a particular word into each entry, it's pretty simple really, and that little trick earlier with the verb to foreign, to fondle, that really was pathetic, yes, of course I don't like writers, there's something so fatuous about some creative people, some artists, who have so much self-belief, how would paul valéry have behaved on that stage, or aragon, or villon, there are three of them in this place with all of us, how many of us are there, let's say fifteen rows and, say, eighteen seats per row, that's two hundred and fifty seats, only half of them are taken, that's a hundred and twenty of us, tops, okay, a hundred and thirty, that's thirty per author, basically a high school classroom full, and all to listen to some guy inventing the verb to foreign oneself, well, mr. yves janvier, you can fuck off think he spoke a foreign language too (sorry, another quote, this time from L. P. Hartley's *Go Between*: "The past is a foreign country: they do things differently there"). 26. The word "Mobutu" means foreigner in Lingala. 27. Marshall Joseph-Désiré Mobutu, dictator of Congo-Kinshasa (and then Zaire) from 1965 to 1997, is therefore General Foreigner. 28. There is also the notion of a Foreign Body. 29. In a poem that refers to "two straight-edged red holes," one is likely to find two foreign bodies inside the individual concerned (a young soldier without a helmet). 30. Similarly, the glasses I am wearing are a foreign body. 31. But the world would feel far more foreign to me without them. 32. Our

and the more I listen to you, to what you have to say, the more you can fuck off, you're just a failed writer, I'd never heard of you before anna mentioned your name, oh, anna, I don't understand you, my anna, my sweetheart, love of my life, what are you looking for, my darling, what sort of myth or fantasy, what sort of dream, all this guy's doing is lining up words and listening to himself talking, he thinks he's so big because he's climbed onto other people's shoulders, giants like camus and terence and who was that other one, and what's this costing per person, this little bit of intellectual masturbation, let's see, each author gets paid what, how much does an author earn, let's say two hundred euros for the evening, I don't have a clue, is that a lot, not a lot, no idea, let's say three hundred euros, so that's a thousand euros for three authors, oh yes, and they've also published a little book, three hundred of them, all numbered, they mention that in the program, let's say two thousand euros for the book, and there's the auditorium rental and marketing, in all it's at least four thousand euros, so every seat that's occupied comes to thirty euros for the state, for the taxpayer, that's outrageous, it really is, but wait, this is corporate sponsorship, bodies harbor a great many foreign bodies: bacteria, viruses, and intestinal flora. They constitute the same volume as a tennis ball. 33. These foreign bodies are our best friends, unlike cancer, which is a little bit of ourselves with a distorted growth rate. 34. A foreigner can be our friend while an intimate acquaintance may be our enemy. 35. If redder means more red then why doesn't foreigner mean more foreign? 36. Try explaining that to a foreigner. 37. Well, to a foreigner who speaks a foreign language, because some foreigners don't speak a foreign language. 38. We can feel closer to some foreigners who speak a foreign language than to certain people who speak our language and are not foreigners. 39. It is sometimes said that speaking foreign languages means you can never be a foreigner. 40. Nothing could be further from the truth: I

this is tax-deductible for the company, and then it makes some great moron in pharmaceuticals feel like, no wait a minute, this is a water treatment company, anyway, the moron feels he's cultured because he's rubbing shoulders with writers, maybe even meeting film actresses, the director from the mining company had a whole load of dancers here, it was postmodern but there was absolutely nothing new about it, we're only on thirty-four and there are seventy-eight of them, we're more than a third of the way through, that's the advantage with numbered texts, you know how much more you've got to listen to, am I being unfair about this, could I actually get into this piece, can I realistically be anything other than angry and jealous, anna, anna, you're intelligent, anna, so beautiful, so attractive, I think you're so gorgeous, more and more with each passing year, surely someone like you who meets hundreds of men, hey, what about weiszbrot last time, that dick weiszbrot danced with you and he really liked you, that was so damn obvious, but you really speak English and feel like a foreigner in London, but don't speak Italian and feel completely at home in Milan. 41. I've always been amazed by the idea that, by taking one step on a mountain peak in the Alps, I can be in a foreign country. 42. But I'm even more astonished that when you cross a border, in the space of a few feet, children start talking a foreign language. 43. I sometimes even feel like a foreigner in my own country. 44. I should probably get used to thinking of the French as foreigners. 45. Who can claim to have an ounce of patriotism left when they come across badly behaved compatriots in a foreign country, and feel ashamed of them? 46. Whichever country you come from, the world still has many more foreigners. 47. I will go one stage further: for some people, the whole world is made up of foreigners. It is if you live

couldn't give a damn, so why this one, then, why does it have to be this one, what is it about him, okay, he's kind of elegant, his voice is quite playful and friendly, his piece is a bit convoluted, it jumps around and it's lighthearted, it's not that bad really, it takes the listener by the hand and it makes you think, but not too much, and it's not trying too hard, I mean it's quite a difficult exercise writing to order like that, and it's easy to listen to, yes, it's pretty okay, not all that literary, not even all that pretentious, either, I was a bit nasty, well, prejudiced, let's say prejudiced, for example I didn't know about mobutu, that's quite a good touch, maybe I could have written this piece if I sat myself down at my keyboard and took the time or maybe that's the writer's secret, making everyone believe they could have written it so that everyone can feel part of it, take it on, and what about me, why have I stopped writing, yes, stopped writing stories, stopped writing poems, writing poems for you, my love, that wasn't bad, was it, do you re-

in Luxembourg: if you get two people from Luxembourg on the same flight from Los Angeles to Chicago, they will be from the same family. 48. Other nations are barely aware foreigners exist. That is certainly the case for Americans, those foreigners who don't even have real names, as Godard would say. 49. The only foreign words that Americans (at least the white Anglo-Saxon Protestant population) know seem to be related to food or clichéd expressions like *la vie en rose*. 50. We should be grateful that foreign words dominate some areas: we are happy to talk about Microsoft in French, it just feels like a name to us, but if you put the word into French, it sounds very limp and unattractive. 51. In the United States, foreign films get their own category. Billy Wilder was cruel enough to say, "Let's shoot a few scenes that are completely beside the point. I want to win the Oscar for the best foreign film." 52. Hearing a French word used in a foreign

member, I wrote a song, a very run-of-the-mill little song, all a bit naive, I'll admit, I should take that up again, I promised myself I'd do it for karl and then for lea, but I didn't do anything, nope, not a thing, time just ate everything up, gobbled it all up but it's not over yet, it's not impossible, I could say to karl, okay, karl, we're going to write down all the stories I used to tell you when you were little, the wonderful adventures of mademoiselle zylliboom the mouse, we're going to make a book, we'll ask lea for some help with the drawings and we'll get help from mommy too, she's really good at writing, your mommy, and maybe mommy and me can make a little sister or a little brother, yes, anna, yes, I know I let the magic slip away, it's my fault, all the laziness and routine got in the way, it's no excuse, we all need surprises in our lives, I'll leave envelopes on the table, in your pockets, in the refrigerator, with poems in language does not make the language feel any less foreign to me, but makes the word feel more foreign in French: *déjà vu* in English or *fauteuil* in German. 53. A foreign language may have a completely different concept of foreignness. 54. The French word for foreigner, *étranger*, is related to the English word "stranger," with the accent on that first *e* representing the long-lost *s* of the original French word, *estranger*. 55. But when Sinatra sang about "Strangers in the Night" we all know he was not talking about foreigners. 56. An English stranger is therefore less foreign than a French *étranger*. 57. In English, you need the word "foreigner" to mean someone from another country. 58. For the one French word, you get two English ones to express degrees of foreignness: the stranger being someone you don't know and the foreigner being someone from a foreign country. 59. There is also the word "outsider," which was used to translate Camus's title

them like in the old days, we'll go back to those walks, to eating crepes on a bench at midnight, we'll do other stuff, I'll think of something, I'll find new things, anna, anna, anna, it can't be, in the second row, I can see the back of your neck, your hair, your dress, you're here, it's you, my head's spinning, my throat feels tight, this hurts, I can't see your face, but I can just imagine your smile, because I know you're smiling, you're smiling at him, really attentive, straining toward him, admiring, no, not admiring, no, but proud, almost worried, I know you, all about you, the way you're looking at him, and there he is talking, reading, to everyone, and to you, I have to go, I can't be seen leaving like a thief, like a cheated husband, like a prick, but I really am a prick, what a prick, I can't breathe, I have to get out, I trip, I get through the door it creaks—leaving already, sir?— yes, I'm leaving, I'm sorry, I, yes, I'm going, the exit is over there,

L'étranger, because the words "stranger" and "foreigner" did not quite fit the bill. 60. Then there is the word "alien," which does not necessarily mean flesh-eating extraterrestrials with antennae; it actually simply means a foreigner: "I'm an alien, I'm a legal alien, I'm an alien in New York," Sting sings. 61. Four English words for the one French one: that gives you some idea how different foreign languages can be. 62. To a man, women can feel completely for-

isn't it, thank you, yes, I can't believe this, I'm all out of breath, I'm out in the courtyard at last, lean against a wall, sit down, that's it, get some air, breathe, breathe, why are you doing this to me, anna, why are you doing this to me, oh, I'm so stupid, this hurts, my heart's exploding, why did I come here, how could I not know, why didn't I get it, why didn't I get it, anna, why are you doing this to me, anna, my anna

eign. 63. As you get to know a woman, she becomes familiar, less foreign. 64. I sometimes wish the women in my life had stayed a bit more foreign. 65 . . .

Yves pauses, has a drink of water.

On the rue de Turenne, Stan walks past his wife's car without noticing it, and hails a taxi.

Yves looks briefly at Anna, and continues.

65. I have thirteen entries left to talk about you under the heading Foreignness: you as a foreigner. 66. But, you see, what I like about you is not that you feel foreign. 67. And I don't think you ever did feel entirely foreign. 68. But I like the fact that something about you still resists, refuses to become familiar, remains invincibly foreign. 69. And it means that when I'm with you, I'm always rubbing up against a foreign element, something mysterious, irreducible, ever present, and full of happiness. 70. Something that might be love's equivalent of

the color of a foreign language in your mother tongue. 71. A little je ne sais quoi, those French words that have passed into so many foreign languages. 72. It makes the way you walk and some of the things you do feel foreign to me for a moment. 73. The curve of your breast, your shoulder, foreign for a moment. 74. Your voice, on the end of the phone, from time to time: foreign. 75. Your perfume, its vetiver fragrance, your own delicate smell: both foreign. 76. Your subtly sinuous thought processes are so foreign to my own meanderings, and yet clearer and sharper. 77. Of course you are not a foreigner, but how I value this foreignness in you. 78. Perhaps keeping that foreign element is the secret.

Yves artfully drops his voice, slows its rhythm, to signal the closing sentence. The reading comes to an end. He gives a wave, the audience applauds, the lights come on and the director of the Heisberg says a few words. When the audience stands up, Anna goes over to Yves, almost running past the rows of seats, she smiles and takes his hand.

"My foreigner," Yves says.

On the rue Érasme, Stan pays for his taxi. He then realizes he has forgotten his bicycle which is still locked up outside the Picasso Museum.

STAN AND ANNA

. . .

WHEN ANNA ARRIVES HOME, it is very late. She has just left Yves and is worried she may have his smell all over her. Even though he has bought her brand of soap for that obligatory shower so a familiar fragrance can protect her from Stan's curiosity. Although she suggested the idea, she still found its realization as crass as it was diplomatic. She has soaped herself scrupulously.

Stan is at his computer.

"Haven't you gone to bed?" Anna asks, amazed.

"No, I was reading *Archives of Ophthalmology*. I was seeing what there was about Fuch's spots. I was waiting for you."

"You shouldn't have. I stayed and had supper with Sarah, from the seminar."

Stan says nothing. Anna's lie is pointless. He would not have asked any questions. He keeps looking at the screen, to avoid looking his wife in the eye.

Anna strokes his hair, affectionately. She still remembers the exact moment she was introduced to Stan, ten years ago now. The mutual friend had joked: "Mr. Stanislas Lubliner, you're looking for a wife, may I introduce Ms. Anna Stein, who's looking for a husband."

Anna laughed as she protested, but when Stan looked at her, shook her hand powerfully yet gently and held her gaze, she immediately thought, Yes, this man could be my husband, the father of my children. That day, she thought she had her future before her, as if she had opened a door onto it.

Stan has been an essential transition, a fording place. She used him to escape the cocoon of her family, and her mother—who finds Stan so irritating—instinctively knows this. Her son-in-law is first and foremost her rival, because Anna used him to break away from her. This evening, at nearly forty, Anna feels that she is still in the middle of that ford.

She takes off her shoes, puts her clothes away in the wardrobe, on automatic. She finds it extraordinary that, having felt such happiness in Yves's arms, she so easily returns to the peaceful family comforts of the rue Érasme. She feels a sense of balance, that's it, a sense of balance.

"With you," she once told Yves, "I'm always going somewhere, moving forward, but I'm not balanced, I'm never stable."

He accepted the image and replied, "There's nothing weird about that. When you're in motion, each instantaneous position is unstable. If you want to be in a stable position, just don't move."

She also told him, "With my husband, I'm on a cruise ship, in first class. Everyone always tells me that."

Yves had no trouble picturing her lounging in a deck chair, surrounded by her family, gazing at the blur of fog along the coast, without ever worrying about pulling up to shore. He wondered whether life actually could be like the teak deck of a steamer. Then she compared him to a sailboat, indulgently granting him the prestige of two masts. The image struck him as rather cruel, but not unfair.

"I don't know," she added, "if it's such a good idea giving up a steamboat for a ketch."

Stan watches Anna moving around the room. He wants to take his wife in his arms, but she would return the hug, and he is afraid he would hold the duplicity against her.

"I'm going to have a shower, my love," Anna says. "I can smell the sweat on me from the day, and I can't stand it."

Stan does not look up.

"Well, I thought you smelled really good."

Anna does not answer. She goes to take her shower, which will help to account for the overpowering smell of soap.

STAN

. . .

STAN IS OLD. The thought cuts through him. When
he looked at his face in the mirror this morning, he
no longer knew himself. Or was it when Anna left, when the
door closed behind her. He thought for the first time that she
could easily not come back one day. He watched at the window
as his wife walked away, then took his coat and went out, he
walked all the way to the Jardin des Plantes. He went into the
magnificent Grande Serre greenhouse, and here he is now,
sitting on a stone bench, not far from the door. He has laid his
hand gently against the bark of a large ficus, as if against an old
friend's lined palm, but all the bark does is stay cold, rough,
and damp, and reiterate in its treelike way: "You're old."

Anna lied to him. She thought she could get away with it,
that is all. But there was a gleam in her eye that he did not recognize, like a moment of truancy betraying her, and to think
she was someone who never wanted to lie. Something in her

eyes had to confess, had to speak for her, and Stan had to spot it so that she could leave without feeling ashamed. As she left, she kissed him that sexless kiss that she so frequently gratifies him with, she turned around and gave him a brief wave. Stan did not hold her back, made no move toward her, he listened to her footsteps dying away in the stairwell. Because of this new shadow, everything was now different and Stan thought that next time he would not bat an eyelid, that Anna could lie and it really would be a lie, because he would not know it.

Stan watches the water drip-dripping along the philodendrons' large cutout leaves. In the early days, before Karl and Lea were born, Anna used to come and meet him when he got off night duty at the Pitié hospital. On the way, she would buy an apple danish and some croissants, she had a thermos full of coffee, and they had their breakfast on this bench in the Grande Serre. There was a building being renovated outside, the work had gone on for two years, and the sound of drills and saws was forever associated with this bench, with the smell of apple from the pastry and the almond taste of Anna's kisses.

At the moment, there is a construction site on the rue Buffon, and the wind carries the creak of cranes all the way here. Stan likes these steel stick insects that prove life goes on, that the city is never finished and keeps moving, that the world changes. The outside air comes in through a window, breezing through his hair, chill as the beginning of winter. Anna must be at the hospital already, the gravel must be crunching under her feet, maybe she is walking quickly, Stan so loves the way she runs, like a big waterbird. Stan listens to the waterfall, the cheeping of finches, he watches the Chinese carp in the pond, the motionless turtles. I love you, Anna, Stan thinks, I'm going to tell you today, this evening, you will listen to me and close your eyes. I want you to close your eyes.

YVES AND THOMAS

. . .

It is with great sorrow that
    Estelle Le Gall,
his wife,
    Thomas Le Gall
his son,
    Jean and Danielle Mousseau-Le Gall,
his daughter,
    Esther, Alice, Aurèle, and Just,
his grandchildren,

    announce the death of
    Pierre LE GALL
    Honorary National Education Inspector

on November 15, 2008, in his eighty-first
year.

A private family ceremony was held at
Saint-Louis Church in La Roche-sur-Yon

This announcement comes with our thanks

It is with great sorrow that
    Jeannine Nordmann,
his wife,
    André Nordmann,
his son,

5 rue des Franciscains
83600 Frejus

    Francis JANVIER
    passed away on November 15, 2008, aged
eighty-three.
    He is buried at the Azelay cemetery, along-
side the ashes of his wife,

    Annie JANVIER,
    née GUERRIN

    Lise Janvier-Butel,
his daughter,
    Yves Janvier,
his son,
    Julie, Françoise, Eliette, his grandchildren

    pay their respects to this
    very special couple.
        We shall speak again in the darkest hour.
                Alfred de Vigny.
12 rue Herold,
75002 Paris

ANNA AND YVES

· · ·

OUTSIDE THE CHURCH, Yves brandishes the announcements page of *Le Monde* at his older sister. Lise is ostentatiously in mourning, veiled hat, black suit, black coat. Her eyes are red and she keeps blowing her nose, noisily. Yves speaks quietly, between his teeth.

"What the hell is this, Lise, this stupid Vigny quote? 'We shall speak again in the darkest hour.'"

"It's a line from *Destinées*," Lise replies curtly. "What did you want, something right-on and witty from Desproges, a bit of Pierre Dac?"[4]

Yves shrugs. He waves the newspaper again.

"And what about 'this very special couple,' where do you get this stuff? Is that our parents you're talking about?"

---

4. Pierre Desproges (1939–1988) was an outspoken and eloquent French humorist. Pierre Dac (1893–1975) was a cabaret singer.

"Absolutely, it's our parents I'm talking about," Lise retorts.
Her voice is a whistle, her mouth spluttering behind her veil.

"Do you know what I think about this, Lise? Do you know
what I think?"

"Oh yes. Very well. I know very, very well."

She would like her brother to stop talking, but can tell he
wants to work right through his anger, so she moves away from
the coffin, which is being carried into the church by four men
dressed in black, as if afraid her dead father can hear Yves. He
turns and follows her.

"So what is it you're telling us with this 'very special couple'?
Are you doing a Disneyland number, is that it? She didn't love
him, she thought he was a dick, she told him so, in front of us,
she gave him a hard time his whole fucking life, and then when
she died, he was left there crying over her . . ."

"She's our mother, you have no right to—"

"I have every right. Horrible people have children too."

"Say what you like. I don't give a damn. God, if you knew
how little I care what you say."

"Yup, I'll say what I like."

"Stop talking so loud in front of . . . the kids . . ."

Lise says nothing more. Her gaze does not extend to the
pretty brunette standing, silently, beside her brother.

Anna understands. She moves away, blends into the small
crowd of people, none of whom she knows and none of whom
want to know her. No distant cousin comes to say hello, no-
body is curious about her. The family keeps its distance from
the son's partner, a bad son who ran away from home so young
and never came back.

Anna was wrong. She wanted to use this painful occasion
to claim her place by Yves's side, she wanted to be beautiful, to

honor Yves. The idea was not inappropriate, but here, in this hostile indifference, she feels too elegant, over-made-up, she wishes she could be invisible. Focusing on his argument, Yves has abandoned her. This anger in him reminds her that even though he no longer wants to be part of a family, he does still have one, and she does not feature in it.

It starts to rain. To the east, over Azelay's slate roofs, a rainbow brightens the sky. If David were here, David, her brother who has "found religion," he would look away from the prism up in the azure, and recite the *Zocher haBrith* blessing to remember the promise the Almighty made not to flood the world again. He would remind her that it was Rabbi Shimon bar Yochai himself, blessing be on him, who forbade contemplating the apparition of a *keshet*, a rainbow, the symbol of God's renewed alliance with man, and that he put a handwritten note about it in the margin of the *Zohar*. But Anna no longer believes in God, she really could not care if the Torah has something to say at any point about waterskiing or whether the glue on postage stamps is kosher. A Jew who loses his or her faith is said to embrace questions because the world is then reduced to endless questioning. Anna looks at the rainbow, without actively defying heaven or its angels.

She steps inside the Gothic church, looks at the statues of emphatically Catholic saints, the brightly colored windows telling the story of Christ's passion, the bust of the Virgin Mary carrying the baby Jesus with maternal bliss, and, looking down the nave, she sees the huge stucco figure of Christ nailed to the cross, *Iesus Nazarenus Rex Iudaeorum*. The coffin is before the altar, draped in black velvet with bouquets of lilies and wreaths of roses laid on top of it, and white candelabras lit around it. Yves no longer believes in God either, but it really is not the same God. Anna inhales the bitter smell of incense and the sickly fragrance of flowers, her head spins, she sits on a pew at the back of the church, shivering, she suddenly feels cold, terribly cold.

She feels like a foreigner. She should not have come. She is not from here. No one will recite the kaddish, *Yitgadal v'yitkadash sh'meh rabba, b'alma di-v'ra chir'uteh,* for the father; no one will tear their clothes before the grave is filled in; no one will lay a stone on the tomb; no one will light a candle in the father's room. No, Anna is not from here, she does not want to be, would never know how to be. She cannot go back to Yves, cannot find refuge in his arms. Everything suddenly seems difficult, almost impossible. They are so different, he is a gentile, she a Jew.

Anna feels like crying. She would like to stand up and walk out of the church, but her legs will not obey her. A man's warm hand takes hers, brings it to his lips. Anna huddles against Yves, the pain is too much for her, it overflows, she cries in his arms, shuddering as she sobs, she wants to stop, but she just can't, she just can't.

THOMAS AND LOUISE

· · ·

*T*HOMAS THOUGHT he would feel no pain. The analyst
believed he was prepared for his father's death, had so
clearly inscribed the idea on his mind that he could already
picture him under the earth. But he has a persistent ache, a
blend of remorse and resentment. He never loved this absent
father, this man he only ever called by his first name, Pierre,
this father who showed so little interest in fatherhood that
Thomas feels he can count the times they spent together on the
fingers of one hand. As a teenager, Thomas wanted to change
his name, he could have called himself Durenne, his mother's
maiden name. Then his anger lost its painful edge, was less of
an issue. Eventually, he even thought he no longer bore him a
grudge.

And yet when, almost twenty years ago now, "Pierre" said
over the telephone, "I know you're hurting, I know you re-
sent me . . . ," Thomas sniggered to himself. He did it loudly

enough for his father to hear, and the freshly qualified analyst in him knew that meant the business was far from over, and he said, "I'm sorry, Pierre. You're probably right. I resented you and I still do."

As he drives to La Roche-sur-Yon, Thomas knows he is going to confront him. If Stoics are right, if there really is nothing between men, no love, tenderness, or friendship, but the body is everything, if all feeling really does germinate and take root in the individual, then this journey, however belated it may be, will not be pointless. Thomas is driving toward his own appeasement.

Louise has canceled all her meetings, she wanted to come with him.

"Thanks for being here, Louise."

Tenderly, without a word, she rests her head on his shoulder, he breathes in her perfume. She closes her eyes, puts her arms around him. She is wearing a sober black suit, looks at the map, acts as copilot.

"We need to take exit 30," she says quietly. "And then the first turn to La Roche-sur-Yon and Noirmoutier."

"In one kilometer, turn left," says the satellite navigation system, which has maintained a discreet silence for nearly five minutes.

"That's what I just said," sighs Louise. "Can't you at least switch it to Italian or Spanish, so we can practice a language?"

"You can actually. You can also have a man's voice, if you like."

"In five hundred meters, turn left onto the D347."

"Someone should invent a GPS for life," Louise smiles, and she adopts the machine's slightly nasal, disembodied voice: "In one week, take a lover. In one day, take a lover. Take Thomas

Le Gall now, on the left. In one month, leave your husband. In one week, leave your husband."

"Leave your husband now," smiles Thomas.

"Turn left now," says the GPS.

"There, you see?" says Louise.

She puts the map down.

"When was the last time you saw your father?"

"Eight months ago, for his eightieth birthday. I hadn't seen him for, what, fifteen years. But I wanted my daughters to meet their grandfather, the 'real' one, at least once. So it wouldn't stay a family secret, a phantom link. They didn't want to, I had to insist and explain, to keep at it. In the end I convinced them by saying that if he died tomorrow, before they got to see him, they'd regret it for the rest of their lives."

"In one kilometer, take the second exit at the rotary."

"You can shut up. So the girls agreed. It was in a big, fancy restaurant, near the Porte Maillot, the sort of place I'm glad I never set foot. It was kind of cheerful, even if I did find it hard relaxing completely. Alice and Esther thought he was very nice, and they loved their cousins."

"Your sister's children?"

"My half-sister's. Aurèle and Just."

"Just?"

"You're right, Just is a weird name. I wanted my girls here for the funeral, but it was too complicated getting them over from Glasgow."

Louise points at a road sign saying LA ROCHE-SUR-YON—15 KM.

Thomas nods.

"I booked a pretty hotel in La Rochelle, in the old town, with views of the sea. We'll leave right after the funeral. Is that okay?"

"Perfect. I have an overnight pass. I said I had to visit a lifer at Saint-Martin de Ré prison, for a review. It's almost true."

"How should I introduce you? Louise Blum? Just Louise? My friend?"

"Yes, Louise is fine, I think. 'My friend' is okay too, seeing I'm here as your friend. And I'm wearing black, which is appropriate."

"Your dress really suits you."

"It's a suit, you moron . . ."

"Take the second turn on the right, onto the D347," intones the GPS.

"Look," Louise says, flipping up her skirt. Bright red lace with gray edging appears right at the top of her naked thigh. "I put on my sexiest underwear. To be honest, I even bought it for . . . for the occasion."

"Fantastic, my love. I'll tell my father as soon as I see his coffin."

Thomas slides his hand onto her knees, strokes her legs and moves right up her thighs, which part to let him through. He slows down, the car shifts a gear.

"Good thing I rented an automatic."

"Turn right now," says the GPS.

Thomas absentmindedly obeys the computer's instructions. His hand slips beneath the silk, flits over Louise's pubis, which proves compliant.

"I love you," says Louise.

Thomas's fingers start to wander, so does he.

"Make a U-turn," the GPS says flatly.

ANNA AND YVES

· · ·

IT IS NOVEMBER and yet summer is still lingering in southern Europe. The French Institute in Florence has invited Yves for a reading of his first book, which has been translated into Italian. Yves takes Anna with him for a long weekend. Their room is very light, with a balcony overlooking the Arno. Anna is watching the river and suddenly spins around.

"Please can we go to Arezzo? I'd really love to see the Piero della Francesca fresco. It's of the Virgin when she is pregnant, she's standing like in Byzantine images of her, impassive, hieratic. She's resting one hand on her stomach, the other on her hip. The colors are gorgeous and her features so fine. They used it in *Nostalghia*, the Tarkovsky film. Do you remember? The poet and the young blond interpreter are driving along in an old Volkswagen. It's pouring rain, the sky's black, it's a winding road and the chapel's right at the top of a hill, surrounded by cypress trees."

Yves thinks he has seen the film, but is not sure he remembers the scene. Anna is insistent: "When they get there, they're celebrating a Mass for the Virgin. The girl goes in alone and the poet stays on the doorstep. The roof has collapsed and the Roman beams are open to the storm. It's raining inside the church, on the flagstones, but the fresco's in an alcove, sheltered from the rain, lit by hundreds of candles. Do you remember?"

Yves wants to remember. Arezzo is in southeastern Tuscany, on the border with Umbria, they will need a car, he rents one.

Anna buys a guide to Tuscany, tries to find the church. With no luck.

Yves makes his inquiries. An hour later, he knows everything.

"Anna, I have bad news."

"The church is closed?"

"It's not that. Your church with the broken roof isn't near Arezzo."

"Really?"

"Yup. It's a Cistercian abbey somewhere near Sienna, San Galgano Abbey. It's so romantic it's been used in several films, like *The English Patient*."

"Is it far?"

"Southeast of Sienna, an hour and a half by car. But you definitely won't see the fresco from the Tarkovsky film there."

"Why not?"

"Because the pregnant Virgin in his film is the *Madonna del Parto*. If you want to see her, you have to go to the Museo de Monterchi, a church not far from Arezzo. Actually, the director chose to film a reproduction of it which is much better quality: the *Nostalghia* Virgin. And that particular Virgin is somewhere else again, in the crypt of a Roman church in San Pietro, in Tuscany."

"I see. Nothing's true."

"Let's say Tarkovsky pieced everything together to make the scene. That's movies for you, make-believe."

Anna says nothing for a moment. When she does speak, her voice is sad.

"You know, that's me all over. The things I want don't even exist, it's all make-believe."

L'abbazia di San Galgano
Dove si trova?
Il complesso monumentale di San Galgano sorge circa 30 km ad Ovest di Siena, al confine con la provincial di Grosseto, fra Monticiano e Chiusdino, in una terra serlvaggia e incontaminata, ricca di bellezze naturali.

Museo della "Madonna del Parto"
Indirizzo: Via Reglia, 1 Monterchi (AR)
Telefono: +39 0575 70713
Orari: Novembre–Marzo, tutti i giorni: 9.00–13.00 e 14.00–17.00
Aprile–Ottobre, tutti i giorni: 9.00–13.00 et 14.00–19.00
Costo dei biglietti:
Intero: 3.50
Ridotto: 2.00 (student oltre i 14 anni)
Ridotto gruppi: 2.50 (gruppi a partire da 15 persone)
Gratuito: ragazzi sotto i 14 anni, donne incinte, abitanti di Monterchi, invalidi e disabili

---

LOUISE AND THOMAS

. . .

*J*UDITH WAS SO FRIGHTENED she is not even crying. Louise is trying to comfort her little girl, but Judith is terrified, she is shaking. There was a screech of brakes, the wheels hit the stroller, but Judith is unharmed. The van stopped with the stroller crumpled under its axle; the doll flew out onto the road. The driver leaped out, a big black man, he just keeps saying to Judith, "You're not hurt, are you? You're not hurt?" He is shaking more than she is.

It is a Sunday in December, the first Louise has spent with Thomas along with Judith and Maud: they have never met him before. Maud discovered that if you say Thomas Thomas over and over it sounds like "stomma stomma stomma." Judith thought that mommy's friend really did have a load of white hair, more than daddy, she chuckled and whispered as much to her older sister, so their mother could not hear.

"What's all this muttering, Judith?" Louise asked.

Judith ran ahead, laughing, she turned to look at her big sister as she started crossing the road. Thomas was the one who saw it coming. He reached out his arm, grabbed the child, and hauled her back. He apologizes to her for squeezing her arm so hard. He hurt her, she gives him a hard time. She's going to have a bruise. The driver has gone to get the doll, has extricated the stroller. It falls apart, is irreparable.

"What's your name, sweetheart? I'll buy you a new one."

Thomas says there is no need, walks him back to the van.

They were meant to go to the Evolution Gallery at the Jardin des Plantes. Louise is completely drained, she just wants to sit down, have a coffee. Thomas asks the girls what they would like. Hot chocolate. Now, that's a good idea. Four hot chocolates.

"Thomas saved your life," Maud tells her sister. Marveling at the enormity of her words, she says them again: "Thomas saved your life."

"What does that mean, mommy, saved my life?" Judith asks her mother.

Louise does not answer. She is hugging her daughter, suffocating her. She looks up at Thomas, closes her eyes, tears glistening beneath her eyelids.

Thomas drinks his hot chocolate slowly. Judith and Maud play with their spoons and the cocoa left in their cups. The fear is forgotten, for a moment. But the terror is gradually working its way through Louise. Thomas can almost read her agitated thoughts. What if Judith had died? She would have left him, most likely. Pain destroys desire, no love could survive guilt like that. She could only have coped with the shared suffering with Judith's father, in fact she would only have wanted to try and overcome it with him.

"Thank you," Louise says eventually.

Thomas shakes his head. In these few minutes of his life, he can see a fork in his own destiny. That was the word Anna used in her last session, when she said, "I don't know whether Yves is my destiny." Coming from Anna, the word was ambiguous, somewhere between freedom of choice and the inevitability of fate.

Thomas does not believe in fate. He would have the power of speech and actions shape our lives. To him, that is the point of psychoanalysis, giving the analysand the strength to become the driving force in his or her own life. If the accident just now had actually happened, he likes to think that, against all the odds, he would have known how to play it right, to become one of the people Louise would lean on.

As a teenager, he had endless discussions about the elasticity of individual fates and History (with a capital *H*, as Perec used to say). The budding Marxist confronted trainee Hegelians. If Hitler had died in a car crash in 1931, would some inertia in the powers that be have doggedly set the war and the Holocaust back on track? Was Stalinism conceivable with a different Stalin? Who could have replaced Trotsky?

Other questions hover. Where did he stand in Louise's story? Did a lover have to turn up at this particular point in her life? Was he interchangeable? Thomas has no idea. He doubts there is some hidden agenda. A breakup has not already happened before the meeting occurs. There are more chance events and contingencies than necessities. Of course, in an ecosystem, occupying the same niche requires the same response: all large marine predators are alike, sharks for the fish, killer whales for mammals, plesiosaurs for dinosaurs. But man is not the natural world, history is not evolution, and Thomas has stopped trying to find a material or scientific answer to a question that could never be either of these. He will never know whether he or Hitler was replaceable, *ersetzbar*. Suffice to say, life never serves up the same dish twice.

Judith and Maud have finished their hot chocolate. They want to go home. So does Louise. They can go and see the thousands of butterflies and the big white whale another time. Louise opens the door to the apartment building, the girls run upstairs. Louise turns to Thomas.

"If Judith had . . . I wouldn't have had the strength for anything, you know. I couldn't have gone on. My life would have stopped."

"No," Thomas says. "No. That's the worst thing, it wouldn't have stopped."

ANNA

. . .

Incomplete list of Anna's purchases.
(from September 8 through December 21, 2008)

One silk dress, size 6, zipper to the side, pleated below the belt, silvery beige, 129 euros.

One pair of pumps in brown faux crocodile leather, size 8, low heel, 79 euros.

One tunic in embroidered cotton, size S, beige and emerald, fastened at the neck, V-neck, embroidery along the neckline and below the bust, flared below the bust, 49 euros.

One black cotton dress, size small, with Navajos pattern, short buttoned sleeves, A-line, 99 euros.

One cotton blouse, size 8, opalescent color, slightly fitted, open pointed collar, sale price 55 euros.

One pair of low-waist jeans, W27 L34, bleached Genoa blue, straight leg, five diagonal-cut pockets including one coin pocket, with leather belt, 89 euros.

One pair of ballet pumps, taupe, small blue tulip on the edging, size 8, 69 euros.

Two silk and polyamide bras, 34B, one in mouse gray and one in bright red with white lace pattern, push-up style with underwiring, hook-and-eye fastening, adjustable straps, 34 euros. Two pairs of "boyshort" underwear in embroidered silk and polyamide tulle, size 8, one in mouse gray and one in bright red, embroidered waistband, 28 euros.

One trench coat, black shot with green, two internal buttons, one belt, wide black leather lapels, size medium, 249 euros.

One pair of black leather sandals, with jeweled ring effect over big toe, two-inch heel, tie-straps at the ankle, size 8, 55 euros.

One one-piece swimsuit, size 8, watermelon pink, deep V-neck with tie at the bust, 49 euros.

One black cotton T-shirt with embroidered neckline, and *Rock 'n' Roll Animal* screen print, 15 euros.

Two pairs of underwear in embroidered tulle (one black, one gray-beige), size 6, 66% polyamide, 25% polyester, 9% elastane, embroidered waistband, 38 euros. Two bras (one black, one gray-beige), 34B, 60% polyamide, 35% polyester, 5% elastane, embroidered, 48 euros.

One pair of taupe-colored, ruched leather boots, round toe, narrow leg, coming high up the leg with diagonal top line, slip-on, size 8, 219 euros.

One chocolate-colored cotton jacket, size 6, single-button fastening, long sleeves, piped pockets, navy blue leather shoulder panels, 99 euros.

One pair of red suede moccasins, white overstitching at the front, low heel, size 8, 39 euros.

One denim skirt, 100% cotton, size small, chalk color, button fastening, zip fly, patch pockets to the side with buttoned flap, small slit to front and back, 59 euros.

One short, low-cut dress in blue cotton, with flounce in navy blue tulle, size 6, 119 euros.

ANNA AND YVES

. . .

IT IS NIGHTFALL. Anna cannot bring herself to leave. She
rests her head on Yves's shoulder, thoughtful.

"My darling goy."

Yves knows full well that Anna calls her husband "my darling." He recognizes the tenderness beneath the irony.

"Do you know what?"

This "Do you know what?" makes Yves smile. It is very often
the pattern that sets off Anna's questioning. He answers every
time without sounding tired of it: "No, Anna, I don't know
what. Tell me."

"You also like me because I'm Jewish." Yves is about to think
this is a ridiculous comment, but she adds: "You would have
liked to be Jewish."

It is a statement of fact.

"Do you mean I regret not being Jewish?" he asks, amazed.

"I do. There's this regret. You've built yourself around it."

Yves does not answer. She takes her idea further: "Being Jewish is an identity. If you could have chosen one, that's the one you would have chosen."

Anna genuinely thinks everyone would like to be Jewish, certainly all writers. Jews all have to do with knowledge and books and handing down memories. A Jew, she says, works hard, wants to pass something on to his children, to leave something for the world. Protestants do too, she concedes, sometimes. But Yves remembers a comment Anna's sister, Nora, made when Anna introduced her to her friend Hugues Léger's work. Nora thought one of his books was magnificent, so perceptive that she could not help a: "Are you sure he's not Jewish?"

It took Anna staring at her in amazement for Nora to start blushing, equally embarrassed to discover her spontaneous assumptions as she was for revealing her prejudices. Yves had nodded, floored, more than a little annoyed.

He wanted to lash out at her: "No, Nora, Hugues Léger wasn't Jewish. Being Jewish isn't a prerequisite for writing a great book. And it's not enough of a qualification either. Would you like me to name some bad Jewish writers?"

But Yves spared Anna's sister. He settled for an ironic smirk, dressing it up in great magnanimity.

And yet Anna never says anything by chance. It is true: Yves would be a good candidate to qualify as a Jew. He is not a philo-Semite, the sort of anti-Semite who loves Jews, but he is interested in Jewishness. He knows a lot about Judaism, its rites and festivals, he listens to klezmer music. Because he speaks German, he understands Yiddish, but who speaks that anymore? He sent Anna a text message for Rosh Hashanah: *A gut yor.* Even though her father was born in Hanover, Anna did not know it meant "Happy New Year." Yves may have become a Trotskyite and a militant, but that was out of visceral antifascism and loathing for the slaughter of the Holocaust, a subject on which he has an impressive collection of books. It is also true that a lot of his friends are Jewish, that he has a particular fondness for Jewish jokes, his favorite being the one about the "alternative."[5] Lastly, he is very aware that he

---

5. *To avoid interrupting the narrative, but not frustrate the reader, the author has allowed himself this footnote.*

One day Moshe goes to see the village rabbi and says: "Rabbi, I've just heard a new word and I don't know what it means. It's the word 'alternative.' What does it mean?"

The rabbi thinks and replies: "Moshe, come back and see me tomorrow with the deeds for the little plot of land down by the river, and I'll answer your question."

The next day Moshe comes back. He has the deeds in his hand. "Right," says the rabbi. "Now you're going to go to the market in Radom, and come back with two rabbits, a vigorous buck, and a young doe."

The next day Moshe is there with his two rabbits in a cage. "All right, Moshe, now listen carefully. You're going to fence off the plot down by the river, where the soil is soft, and you're going to put your rabbits in there. In a few months you'll have twenty young rabbits, you can sell half of them in the market, and reinvest the rest of the money to buy the neighboring plot, which you will also fence. By the end of the year you will have bought all the land along the river up to the bridge and you'll be the richest man in the village. You'll carry on with your business and your investments, buying up all the plots on both banks and down the valley, all the way to the village of Brentsk, and you'll be one of the most prominent men in the region. You will marry young Sarah—oh, don't deny it, Moshe, I've seen the way you look at her—so you'll marry young Sarah then, and she'll give you two beautiful children, a boy and a girl. Meanwhile, you'll carry on breeding thousands of rabbits, selling them in the market in Radom, Piotkrow, and Kativice, and you'll be rich, very rich. Your children will grow up, your daughter will start seeing the doctor in Lublin, the boy will start studying at Lodz. And then, Moshe . . ."

"Then, Rabbi?"

"Then the water level in the river will rise, an incredible flood, you'll lose everything, the land will be carried away, the rabbits will drown in their thousands, you'll be ruined, your wife will leave you, cursing you for your lack of foresight, your children will refuse even to speak to you, and you'll end up drunk and penniless like a poor schnorrer. That's what will happen."

"But Rabbi. I don't understand. You were supposed to tell me what 'alternative' meant."

The rabbi thinks for a moment and says: "The alternative, Moshe? The alternative is ducks."

has fallen in love with more Jewish women than statistics could have predicted.

"Okay, you're never going to be Jewish Writer of the Year," a (Jewish) friend once told him, "but why don't you go for the Goy Novel Prize?"

For all that, does Yves regret not being Jewish? Saying no would start Anna analyzing his reaction as a denial. Yves wants to find a suitable answer to this question he has never asked himself. He is probably an indeterminate cocktail of Gaul, Viking, and Goth, but he has never hated the insecurity of having no clear provenance, like a wine's *appellation contrôlée*, never wanted to wear another man's shoes. He has built himself around a refusal to belong, a rejection of family. He likes the fact that his mother tongue sometimes feels foreign to him. He would like to give Anna a precise answer. As soon as the conversation turns to Jews, or worse, to Palestine and its "territories" (a word she does not always qualify with "occupied"), to "terrorism," he is always on thin ice. The subject is so close to Anna's heart that she sometimes loses all sense of judgment. She once let slip a "You French people," which riled Yves, particularly as she would have left him for a "You Jews."

Yves takes the leap: "To be absolutely honest, Anna, I'm glad I'm not Jewish. If I'd been born Jewish, I might have settled for that. That whole illusion of being something is so intoxicating. I could have been one of those kids in a yarmulke demonstrating with a PROUD TO BE JEWISH sign. Do you really think you can feel proud just for being born Jewish? That's just as stupid as saying you're proud for being French."

"No. It's not the same. Jewish culture is five thousand years old."

"Hey, that's enough fictionalizing, Anna. Two thousand eight hundred at the outside. And being a Jew today isn't like it was under Ptolemy or Caesar."

"Those kids don't have to hide, they don't have anything to be ashamed of."

"That's not the point. Everyone, whether or not they're Jewish, can be proud of Jewish culture. Everyone has a right—a duty, even—to be, just as they should be proud of everything the human mind has achieved. When I walk through the Alhambra, I'm very proud of Muslim culture."

"Really? I didn't know you were such an ecumenical slob with regard to religions."

She is right. Yves loathes religious figures, Jewish ones as much as any other. In churches, Prévert used to say, there is always something that does not ring true. But he is happy to acknowledge the universal qualities of Judaism. When he read his piece about foreignness, he omitted an idea he wanted to keep for another text. It was that in Hebrew, becoming a Jew was called *leitgayer*, which means "become *ger*," become a foreigner, because the Jews were foreigners in the kingdom of Egypt. So the temptation to become something else is inseparable from Jewish culture. Anna would most likely retort that he was philosophizing, that *leitgayer* simply meant becoming a guest, a guest of the Jews. But *ger* is less ambiguous in biblical Hebrew, he had talked to a rabbi about it: it means "foreigner," period. Nothing sacred can be achieved without being aware of this rootlessness. The tribe of Levi had no right to own land for that very reason: a priest is a living emblem of people who are never completely at home.

Yves's mischievous side could almost say that, in order to conceive the world properly, you have to conceive it as a Jew would, as someone from nowhere and who owns nothing would. But he is pretty sure he has already said that to Anna, and he would rather not repeat himself.

"Look, Anna, I'm just saying that being under the illusion of being Jewish because your mother is, doesn't really mean being Jewish anymore. Being born Jewish is nothing. You can't cut corners to become one."

"More sophistry. Sophistry that conveniently forgets about the pogroms, the persecutions, the Shoah."

"I'm not forgetting anything, Anna. But saying Einstein and Freud were Jewish geniuses means thinking the same way as the Nazis."

Yves is getting carried away, so he can tell that Anna has touched a nerve, that actually, yes, if he really did have to choose some mythical connection, then maybe. But there would be other possible options. Anna shrugs her shoulders, she does not want a fight.

"But it's true, Freud and Einstein *were* Jews. Look, I'm bored of this, it's beside the point. You haven't answered my question."

Yves says nothing, amazed at his own clarity. In the past, when a situation was too tense, his mind fogged over, bombarded with parasitic images. At fifteen, he would lose the thread of his thoughts during family arguments because he would suddenly have an absurd mental picture of a Galápagos turtle laying an egg. He would lose the ability to argue his point, even when he knew he was right. It took him some time to realize that this stupid habit was a symptom, that it derived from his inability to face up to things completely.

"Anna, I'm going to give you one last reason why I'm glad not to be. If I were Jewish, I'm not sure our relationship could have happened."

Anna says nothing in reply. She remembers that, during one of her sessions when she mentioned that Yves was a goy, Le Gall asked: "Could you have fallen in love with a Jew?"

She sat there in silence. Le Gall had asked the right question, though. The fact that Yves was a goy made everything easier. Sneaking into another Jew's bed would have been obscene, it would have meant betraying the union blessed by the synagogue. Yves was from another universe, parallel and exotic. His world coincided so little with hers that it was barely a scratch on the marriage contract.

LOUISE AND ROMAIN

· · ·

AN AUSTRALIAN BIRD, called the superb lyrebird, can imitate any sound, from the noise of a diesel engine to a jackhammer. That afternoon, it would only have taken a dozen of them to reproduce the sounds of Paris.

Louise feels light, suspended in air, in love. If she really is leaving Romain, it is for this forgotten sense of lightness. The sky is an infinite gray. It somehow manages to hide the sun and the shape of the clouds. Louise would like a brighter sky, an Argentine blue. She went to Buenos Aires five years ago, and the name will always remind her of the blue of the sky slicing between apartment buildings.

The signs say TRADITIONAL BAKERY, NEWSAGENTS & LOTTERY, CRÉDIT AGRICOLE BANK. That rural word "Agricole" stranded in a city does not strike her as incongruous. Louise has always liked the adjective "incongruous," because it is itself incongruous. On the bus stop there is a poster for an American film with Nicole Kidman, another one for a German sedan; it flips over to make way for a Korean cell phone. Louise is traveling across Paris to leave Romain, yet she is looking at advertisements. She draws energy from the light in the sky, the glistening leaves and shifting branches. She looks at posters, some workmen digging a trench through concrete, boutiques, dresses, and ankle boots. She is going to leave Romain and yet she is looking at dresses and ankle boots.

She has put on her makeup and this black dress which—she knows for sure—really suits her. She is wearing that ivy and sandalwood perfume that Romain gave her for her birthday, the one that is too woody and precious for her. She does not know why she took so long getting ready, when it would have been far more tactful to have made herself as plain as possible, to have tried to be as unattractive as possible. She wonders whether she has gone to all this trouble for him or for herself.

She knows that there are men on café terraces looking at her, right now, as she walks up the Boulevard Saint-Germain. Any woman walking through Paris may, at any given moment, have a man looking at her.

She is heading off to leave Romain. She will have the courage to tell him that she actually left him a long time ago. She is walking through Paris to demonstrate that the thread between them has broken, that she is tied to him by the children, but that can never be enough. She can no longer see herself by his side. She has already forgotten the happiness that, only yesterday, she felt beside him.

First, Louise made mental lists, lined up columns. She put together a grid as logical as the blocks in an American city. One column *For Leaving Romain*. One *Against*. Or rather, she no longer loves him the way she ought to love him to keep on loving him.

As she filled in the lines, she could have written: the way you sometimes smile, the slightly English way you have of looking bored, your slightly bitter humor, your green eyes that are sometimes gray, your long thin hands. The *For* and *Against* columns would have been full of the same words; she realizes that what once attracted her puts her off now. The almost feminine charm that seduced her no longer has any effect on her, what she wants now is fiercer. The shy way he stroked her, that she used to find so arousing, exasperates her now, she needs passionate urgency.

Louise has also made a list of their differences. At the movies, Romain always chose a seat at the back of the theater, but she preferred being close to the screen. They took buses 30, 31, 53, 27, and 21, and Romain developed incredible strategies to get seats for them both. Louise was quite happy to stay standing. They did their shopping at Franprix, Carrefour, and Monoprix, and Romain had a logical way of filling the grocery cart: not one squashed strawberry, not one crushed baguette. Louise could never manage it. They argued about bread being over- or underbaked, about the war in Iraq which should or should not have been fought, about painting the bedroom; Romain gave way with a sigh every time: it didn't matter. Louise doesn't know what *does* matter.

Yes, Louise has made lists, it is her way of organizing her life.

With Romain, she liked the smell of cut grass beside the pond in the Jardin du Luxembourg, even though she is allergic to cut grass. She liked the mermaid on the barge gliding beneath the Passerelle des Arts, and the wind lifting her skirt. She liked the cold wind of a Siberian depression blowing across Place Blanche one morning, even though she does not like the cold, or Place Blanche. She liked the pink of a sunset from the top of the park at Buttes Chaumont, creasing up her eyes to look at it. She liked the taste of her too-hot hot chocolate in a café on the rue des Abbesses, even down to how much the scalding hurt. She liked all of that, and Romain was there, with her, right when she liked it. She wonders whether she liked it because he was there.

Romain is waiting for her in a bistro on the rue Montmartre, he is drinking a cup of coffee.

It was Louise who told him that *bistro* means "quick" in Russian, that the French word dates back to the occupation in 1815, when Russian soldiers asked for a drink *bistro, bistro,* before their officers arrived. Romain told her that the Japanese were going to modify coffee genetically so it no longer had any caffeine in it (or so it had more caffeine, she does not remember). Louise told him that the oldest house in Paris is on the rue de Montmorency, that the alchemist Nicolas Flamel lived there (or died there). Romain told her that Mouton-Duvernet was a general and Denfert-Rochereau a colonel (or perhaps it was the other way around). In ten years they had told each other a lot of things: Louise has not remembered much of it, Romain a great deal more.

Romain will already have ordered her coffee.

He will probably be worried, will sense that Louise's already absent-sounding voice foreshadows her imminent absence. At first he will refuse to hear what she is saying, then he will want Louise to say she is sorry but she has to go, to prolong that final moment, for time to stretch out like a wave; he would like Louise's words alone to be enough to keep her there as if, terrified by the weight of what she is saying, she will suddenly find she cannot leave.

But Louise will find the opening words and the ones that come next. She has a solution to everything, the children, the apartment, she has thought of everything. He will ask her to give him one chance, he will say he is going to change, that everything can start again. She will say it's not about him. It's her.

YVES

. . .

*Y*VES HAS STARTED WRITING AGAIN. He has read that in
Abkhazia, a small former Soviet republic on the Black
Sea, they play dominoes like nowhere else. First, they use
as many sets of twenty-eight dominoes as there are players, less
one. One set for two players, two sets for three players, etc. Most
importantly, in Abkhazian dominoes, any tile put into the chain
can be removed and played again. Which is what happens when,
for example, a player can no longer play any of his tiles even after
two turns drawing from the talon. Once a tile has been removed,
there are then two chains which can be played indiscriminately.
Also, any player who holds a double is allowed to lay it down and
start an independent chain. It is a very complex game in which
bluffing is allowed, and it ends when there are no dominoes left
in the talon. The average game lasts a long time.

Yves wants to write a novel around six characters. He will associate each of them with the numbers on dominoes, with the

blank applying to a secondary character, though never the same one. The novel will reproduce the trajectory of a game of Abkhazian dominoes: every double played will give rise to a chapter with just one character, a tile with two different numbers to a chapter with two characters, very occasionally three if one of them says and does nothing. Double zero is an interesting case: it will produce a chapter with two secondary characters, or just one. Yves has chosen a game between two teams of two players, played in 1919 at a tournament in Sukhumi. It is a famous game because it lasted two hours, the 1-3 and 2-6 tiles were reused several times, and three chains were formed. The Abkhazian writer Dmitry Iosifovich Gulia mentions it in his *Apsny*, the diary he kept in the 1920s. Yves's novel will be called *Abkhazian Dominoes*, but nothing about its structure will be explained to the reader. Particularly as Yves ends up never entirely respecting his own rules.

When he described how it would be put together to Anna, she shook her head: "Too complicated. Pointless. My darling goy, you really do go to great lengths to make sure your books don't sell. And as for the title, it's kind of hard to remember."

"No it isn't. 'Abkhazian' is intriguing and dominoes are child's play."

"Not with you on that. Make it simple. Is your book about love?"

"Yes."

"Well, put 'love' in the title."

One day, in a bookstore, Yves recognizes one of his poetry collections stacked in a pile by the register, with a little handwritten card saying: BOOKSELLER'S CHOICE. Amused, he points it out to Anna discreetly.

"You see, I do sell a few."

Anna is delighted. Without a moment's hesitation, she tackles the proprietor with: "Do you know you have the author himself standing before you?"

Yves is dumbstruck. He could smile about it, absently, extricate himself with a joke, but he just wants the ground to swallow him up. He is reliving the "Kennedy affair" and his mother's stifling pride. He would have hoped to have grown out of that.

Anna wants him to be more outgoing, more dazzling. She is actually less eager for him to be successful than for him to want to be successful.

"If you were famous," she once admitted to him, not without shame, "I would probably be with you already."

He shook his head, dispirited. He remembers the verdict given by a British friend who collects vintage cars and alimonies, after he had introduced him to Anna: "My dear, that girl's a Bugatti. A lot of maintenance."

Some days, nothing is right. It can be a painting on the wall ("a bit crass"), a book on a shelf ("Please don't say you liked it"), four cans of spaghetti in a cupboard ("I don't believe it, that's a bit obsessive-compulsive"), or the way Yves twists the spoon around in his mouth when he eats yogurt ("taking far too much pleasure in it"). And if Yves drives a little too quickly for her liking for a moment, she sighs, "How could I ever trust you with my children?"

Anna would so like to be able to admire him, the way she admires Stan, his scientific earnestness, his respect for patients, his work on retinas "that's going to save thousands of people," she is convinced of it.

Because Stan is infallible, he cannot help but be infallible. And the tiniest disillusion destroys her: one Sunday afternoon Stan is cooking with the children, making a cake known as a four-by-four—four eggs, 250 grams of flour, 250 grams of butter, and (fatal slip) 250 grams of salt . . . When the cake comes out of the oven it looks different. Anna tastes a bit and immediately spits it out, making a face and flying into such a disproportionate rage that the children run to their bedroom for refuge. She talks about it in her session with Le Gall two days later, shattered to find tears welling in her eyes again as she relates the incident.

Thomas felt Anna had had enough that day. The analyst was afraid she would leave Stan, that she would go ahead and do it even though, at that stage, she could only go from one father figure to another, because all there was room for in her was fathers and lovers. Yves belonged only to the second category. Le Gall took the unusual step of warning her: "Sometimes, Anna, changing men means actually not changing at all."

As on every other Thursday morning, Yves was waiting for Anna when she emerged from the session. She told him what had been said, and he felt just how right Le Gall was, how unprepared she was to make this leap. And Yves, who wanted her so desperately, could almost have thanked the analyst for holding her back.

Yves is often irritated by Anna's demands. She is so afraid of "becoming poor" with him. The day she admits this, he looks at her, lost for words, says that the fear is ungrounded and that—more than anything else—the very thought of it is beneath her, but she presses the point, genuinely worried: "I need security. I can't live without it. It's neurotic. I'm trying to work on it. Don't hold it against me, please. Do you want to know the exact word? Living with you, I'd be scared of . . . of decline."

Decline: "fall," "degeneration." Yves sighs at the cruelty of synonyms.

They agree on nothing. Yves has not shaken off every element of the Trotskyite he was as a teenager, Anna says she loathes Alter-globalizationists. One day when Yves is defending them over dinner, Anna's temper flares immediately: "No society can have equality as its aim. Look what happened when they did try for equality. People just aren't equal."

Yves is on home territory with his reply: equality is not an aim at all, but the means to ensure that the best shine through, overcome their condition. Why, if "money is a driving force," does she only admire artists, experts, and writers? She digs her heels in, they argue. The other people around the table calm things down.

When Yves is alone in the kitchen with an old friend for a moment, he smiles and says: "You must be wondering what I'm doing with that woman, or what she's doing with me."

"No," the friend says evenly, although his eyes do seem to be mulling something over. "You're just very different. A positive pole and a negative pole."

Another thing Anna says is, "Nothing is ever good enough for me. You'll hate me for that. It's really frustrating for a man if nothing he does is ever good enough for a woman."

Yves cannot argue with this point. It takes considerable effort on his part to allow himself to believe that, in spite of everything, Anna could gain from the situation.

One day, when he was seriously irritated, he looked through his bookshelves for Drieu La Rochelle's book *A Woman at her Window*, so that Anna could read these superlatively reactionary, misogynistic words: "Women, who are always ingrained with a powerful realism, can only ever love men for their strength and prestige."

"There. Do you really want that bastard Drieu to be right?"

"But that's exactly the way it is," Anna snapped. "You're impossible. Look at you: you have a first-class ticket in your pocket but you prefer traveling second-class or staying on the platform."

"I can't stand the people in the first-class compartment. If you love me, come and join me in second-class."

Yves loathed having to string out the metaphor. He thought it was full of pitfalls. If life were a train, who was dodging the fare in first-class, who was checking the tickets? It was bordering on the absurd, he did not want to take it any further.

And yet Anna drives him to change himself. After all, if success makes no difference, then why not be successful? He is not sure he has the profile for it. Every time he hears a note of admiration from the person talking to him, she kisses him. He feels sullied by it, wants to shrug it off like a dog shaking itself after the rain. He feels like an impostor. Feels the whole world is full of impostors.

But he has started writing again, and *Abkhazian Dominoes* is taking shape. Of course, Anna is not wrong. Why should the layout of a book obey a weird and universally forgotten game of dominoes? Yves smiles. And carries on building the edifice, all the more obstinately.

THOMAS AND ROMAIN

. . .

A T 5 PM IN HIS APPOINTMENTS DIARY, Le Gall has written "Fabien Dalloz," and that is exactly the time when the new patient, whom he has never met, rings the bell. As he opens the door to him, Thomas says smoothly: "Fabien Dalloz? Thomas Le Gall. Please come in."

The man does so and, despite his tremendous height, it is only when Romain Vidal has sat down in the armchair that Thomas recognizes him. Of course: Roman—Fabian, that part's clear, but getting from Vidal to Dalloz is a job for the dictionary.

Thomas sits down at his desk, opposite Louise's husband. He thinks briefly of admitting that the ruse has fallen flat, a move that becomes more arduous with every passing second. But the familiarity of his setting and the effect of the surprise make him instinctively pronounce the usual words: "I'm listening."

At first Romain says nothing. Not for a moment does Thomas imagine this is a coincidence, that Vidal is in this

room for a consultation: Louise has talked to him, and Romain
has come to measure up the man who wants to take his wife
away. By simply changing his name, he thinks he holds all the
cards. But sooner or later Le Gall and the real Romain Vidal
will have to meet, and when the time comes to leave the analyst's office, the false Fabien Dalloz will have no choice but to
drop his mask.

Silence settles between them, and Thomas respects it. He
does not want to insist that Louise's husband speak frankly
right away.

"I don't know how to start. I don't know where to start,"
Romain blurts eventually.

Always start at the end, Thomas does not say. If you think of
life as a book, you'll never be able to see where it finishes.

Essentially, however strange it may seem, this conversation
might be not unlike a normal session. A man comes to see
another man, with a secret that is not entirely a secret, one he
will have to consent to disclose. A man who often says nothing.

"Right," Fabien-Romain says briskly. "In a nutshell, I'm
married, we have children, two children, my wife's met someone, and she said she's leaving me. It's pretty straightforward.
I'm very . . . unhappy, but I don't think having analysis is the
answer. It takes years, doesn't it, but it's right now that my
wife's leaving."

Romain stops talking. Thomas opens a notebook, jots down
a few words to create a semblance of composure, but can keep
the pretense up no longer: "You're Romain Vidal, aren't you?
I'm sorry but playing cat and mouse isn't a very good idea."

Romain looks at him, then lowers his eyes and stares at the
foot of the desk lamp. His whole face closes in, his breathing
accelerates. Thomas stands up to break away from an analyst's

typical aloof, seated position. He walks over to the window, gently tilts the slats of a blind. He is waiting for Romain to give in to his anger, his sorrow. As Louise's husband stays locked in silence, Thomas toys with the blind, smirking as he cannot help thinking this sort of blind is also known as a *jalousie*—a jealousy.

"I can understand why you're here," he says. "I felt the same curiosity, to see who you were. I went to one of your conferences."

An ambulance passes outside, barely audible through the door. Thomas lets it pass, the sound fades.

"As you're here in my office, you must be expecting something from this meeting. But I don't know what. You haven't come to ask me to stop loving Louise."

"I—I don't th-think so," Romain murmurs, possessed by his teenager stammer.

"You're here to put a face to your fears. That's a good enough reason."

Thomas stays looking at the sky, the trees in the courtyard. He is probably not who Romain was expecting.

"You don't understand. By confronting me here, in this particular place, you're trying to find the strength to win Louise back. But I'm five years older than you, ten years older than Louise; in other words, I'm old. You're brilliant, famous even. So why me? It's almost worse."

Romain has looked up again. Thomas is still waiting for him to speak, but Romain gazes at motes of dust twinkling in rays of sunlight. The analyst continues, calmly, through a silence punctured by the least noise. "You're looking at your shattered life as if it were someone else's. You're hurt, humiliated. You've lost your self-esteem. That's what most people feel."

Between each of his sentences, Thomas establishes a pause, leaves a space he would like Romain to fill. But Vidal cannot do it.

"You know, dozens of people have been through this room. People full of pain. My job is to step up and tackle that pain with my own experience of pain. My own pain, Romain, is grief, from a long time ago."

Thomas has removed any emotion from his voice. By using Romain's first name, he hopes to extract a response, but the man shows no reaction.

"I know nothing about you," Thomas goes on. "That's why what I'm about to say may not apply to you. Often, when a man wants a woman, it gives her a mysterious charm to other people. I'm not casting any doubt on the sincerity of—"

"Shut up."

Thomas stops talking. They stay like that for a long time, not saying anything. The doorbell rings. The six o'clock appointment is early. Romain unfolds his great body, which seems to be a burden to him today. Thomas follows him, opens the door of his office. At the last moment, Romain turns around. Thomas looks at the hand held out to him, amazed; shakes it. Romain's handshake is genuine.

All he says is: "Maud told me. About Judith." The giant's throat constricts. He cannot get the words "Thank you" out.

ANNA AND MORAD

. . .

"WHAT DOES 'UPSET' MEAN?"
A little boy asked Anna this question.

Sometimes, on the way home from the hospital, Anna makes a slight detour and drops in on Yves, staying for an hour, or two. She tells him about her day, the patients, the progress they are making. That day, a woman had come to see her with her five-year-old son. It was their tenth visit, she is from Mali, very young, speaks French badly. Her little boy Morad is very restless, has trouble concentrating; it was his nursery school that asked for him to be seen. He sat, quietly, drawing with colored pencils, a tree, a path, in dark shades. Within a few sessions a difficult truth emerged: the mother had never dared tell the child that his father died on a building site two years ago. All she had managed was to say, Daddy's not here anymore, he's gone. This absence filled the child with unutterable shame, as he pretended to wait, in vain, for his father to come back, although he had probably grasped the truth. His mother—powerless and overwhelmed—clung stubbornly to her lie. She thought she could protect her son, distance him from that suffering, but it was from herself that she was distancing him: Morad was alone in his distress.

Anna went on the journey with the mother and child as they took the first steps toward this revelation. All of a sudden, the words were said, and Morad looked at his mother in amazement. It was when Anna told Morad, "Now when you're upset you can talk to mommy about it," that the child asked his question.

"What does 'upset' mean?"

"Sad. Do you know what it is to be sad?"

The child nodded. Anna looked at him, smiled, and said: "Do you remember your father, Morad?"

The child did not answer. The mother had tears in her eyes.

"What about you," Anna said, turning to her. "What could you tell Morad about his father? What sort of thing did he like doing with Morad, for example?"

The mother thought for a long time, then murmured: "My husband liked singing. He sang a song, a song from our village."

"And do you still sing this song with Morad?"

"Oh no, I don't sing it. I can't sing."

"How about you, Morad, can you sing?"

The child looked at his mother, drew a little bear. Anna did not give up.

"Would you agree to sing the song for us?" she asked the mother. "Maybe just the tune?"

The woman consented, squeezing her handkerchief in her hand, silent. Her knuckles went pale. She sang softly, but it took considerable effort.

"*Aandi d'beyyib ya mahleh ya mahleh gannouchou khachmou wateh.*"

"What's the song about?"

"It means: 'I have a little teddy bear, soft and cute, with an adorable nose . . .'"

"So, do you remember it at all, Morad? If you're sad, maybe you and mommy could sing the song your daddy used to sing when you were a little baby."

The child smiled at Anna and nodded his head. Yes, he knew the song, "*Aandi d'beyyib ya mahleh.*" He would sing it with his mommy. For his daddy who's dead. He got it. "*Aandi d'beyyib ya mahleh.*" He was allowed to be upset. Now he knew he could turn to his mother once more, to talk about his father. The mother would be back in her rightful place. She could cope with it now.

Yves listens to Anna. He feels a surge of tenderness, and goes to make a cup of tea before Anna notices the tears in his eyes and makes fun of him.

YVES AND STAN

. . .

*T*HERE ARE NOT MANY PEOPLE left in the More or Less Bookstore, and Yves is about to get up from the table where he has been doing signings and join the manager at the register. A man approaches, Yves has not spotted him, he has been waiting until the very last moment to come over: he hands him a copy of *Two-Leaf Clover*.

"Who is it for?" Yves asks.

"To Stanislas and Anna, please. Anna is my wife."

The tone of voice is not very friendly. Yves looks up, quickly appraises the man. He is tall, early forties, wearing horn-rimmed glasses. His brown cord jacket is like the one Anna tried to get him to buy just three days ago. Of course this Stanislas right here is Anna's husband, he knows everything, this moment had to happen. Perhaps he has seen them together, perhaps a friend has tipped him off.

Yves wants to buy some time.

"You did say Anna, not Hannah with aitches?"

"No aitches."

"To Stanislas and Anna . . ." Yves writes, then he says: "I'm sorry, but do we know each other?"

"No," Stan replies. "I'm sure we've never spoken."

Stan's voice is cold, hostile. He opens and closes his fist, agitatedly. Anna once told Yves that if Stan ever found out about the two of them, he might "smash his face in." He warned Anna: if her husband insulted him, he could accept that, but at the first punch, he would press charges.

The punch never comes. Neither does the bland but subtle dedication appropriate for these exceptional circumstances. Yves merely writes this frequently quoted sentence, borrowed from Diotima in Plato's *Banquet* and ably transformed by Lacan who then appropriated it:

> . . . a story of love, that thing we give without ever possessing it.
>
> Yves Janvier

He hands the book to Stanislas, who glances briefly at the dedication. He is not the man Yves imagined he was. Anna definitely described him the way a child describes her father, overestimating everything. Stan was "very tall": Yves smiled when he discovered his actual height. It was the same as his. Stan pulls up a chair, sits down close to him.

"I've just read one of your books. *Follow On*, is that what it's called?"

His voice is deep, Yves finds it melodious.

"Yes, it's a short novel, quite old now."

"Your writing is very, how shall I put this? Very fluent."

Yves wrote *Follow On* fifteen years ago. The story of a man with a lot of time on his hands who, out of curiosity, starts following a woman in the street. He takes pleasure in walking behind her every day. At first the book is built around the notes he makes. He spies on her when she does her shopping or goes for a walk with her children or her husband. Weeks go by. He decides to try and seduce her: he is charming and intelligent, he succeeds, and when the woman falls, becomes infatuated with him, separates from her husband, quite irretrievably, he is suddenly afraid, he leaves her and disappears. Having ravaged the woman's life.

It is crystal clear where Stan is going with this.

"It isn't a portrait of a woman, even though it does describe her the whole time. It tells us about a man through the way he sees a woman. What's his name again?"

"Kostas. And the woman is Camille," says Yves.

"Kostas, that's right. Camille has a husband and children, she's happy. The more he watches her life, the more he realizes how alone he is. It's her happiness he falls in love with. But he doesn't really love her."

"I don't know. I think he does."

"No, wanting someone isn't the same as loving them, Mr. Janvier. He doesn't measure the consequences of what he does to this woman's life, to her children. He's not interested in that, his intentions are egotistical. It's a portrait of a bastard."

"Why a bastard?"

"Kostas would have every right if he knew for sure what he really wanted. But he doesn't, he has his doubts, is torn, and he knows that. Being sure of what you actually want, that's the bare minimum you'd expect of yourself if you're about to break up a marriage, making a woman—and her children—suffer. Wouldn't you say?"

"Yes. Perhaps. Kostas is a bastard in spite of himself."

Stan opens and closes his fist, his knuckles go white.

"A bastard in spite of himself is still a bastard. There is something fragile about Camille, a dissatisfaction with things. But she has a good life. Perhaps too good. Camille carries a deep-seated melancholy in her, and her husband helps her carry it, very tenderly. When Kostas turns up, she hopes she can actually live, at last. Kostas can tell she is vulnerable, he also suspects she loves him because he embodies unpredictability, a sense of adventure she always longed for, but he exploits her dreams to draw her in. It's a woman thing, like Emma Bovary meeting her Rodolphe. Very traditional, in fact. But you're too understanding with Kostas. You adopt his point of view. There are several novels that need writing there, Camille's, her husband's, the children's. Those are the ones you should have written."

"They're tragic novels. I . . ."

"Well, maybe *Madame Bovary* can't be written more than once, after all."

There is a note of sadness in Stan's voice, but no longer any anger. He is still rubbing his fist against his palm, but talking seems to have soothed him. The bookstore is gradually emptying and the manager signals discreetly to Yves.

"Do you have children, Mr. Janvier?" Stan goes on.

"A daughter. Her name is Julie."

Stan shakes his head.

"Anna and I have two, you know. I read every page of *Follow On*, imagining a Kostas following Anna, meeting her, seducing her. It made me really sad to think a man that immature, who did so little to deserve her trust, could come and destroy my Anna's life, hurt our family, for nothing, just because he never really gauged what he wanted."

"I understand what you're saying."

"I know you understand what I'm saying. There's a bit of Camille in every woman, and a bit of Kostas in every man."

Stan stops talking for a moment. Yves flicks his pen back and forth between his fingers. He does not want to argue; he is moved by Stan, more than he expected. Anna's respect and affection for Stan hatched a peculiar empathy in him some time ago. Yves now knows that the love two men feel for the same woman weaves secret connections, even forbidding that lover's privilege, jealousy.

"I'm sure I wouldn't write the same book now."

"Do you think? Yet they say people always write the same book."

"It's not true. Books are like the days of your life. They come one after another and you learn from each of them."

"Well . . . that's a good thing, then. That's a good thing."

"Kostas doesn't want to make anyone unhappy."

Stan gives a furious shrug and stands up. Yves stands too.

"That's not possible, Mr. Janvier. People like Kostas aren't happy and they can't make anyone happy."

All at once Yves feels cold, puts on his coat. Stan gives a slight bow and steps away.

"I'm very glad I've had a chance to meet you, Mr. Janvier. To talk about Kostas and Camille with you. I hope I haven't bored you."

Yves shakes his head. Stan walks off without offering a handshake. Before he leaves the bookstore, he opens the book, leafs through it. He comes back, looking determined, fists balled. From the look in his eye, Yves can suddenly tell they are going to fight. He prepares for it. Deep down, he prefers this to their restrained discussion in which they both affected detachment. But Stan simply shows him the dedication.

"Excuse me. You wrote 'To Stanislas and Anna.'"

"Yes?"

"My name's Ladislas, not Stanislas. Could you write 'To Ladislas and Anna'?"

Yves is dumbstruck. He apologizes, takes another copy, and corrects his mistake. Ladislas walks away, satisfied. The manager smiles at the writer, slightly dismayed: "I'm so sorry, Yves. I should have warned you. Ladislas is a regular. He's—how shall I put this?—a bit different. One time, when Delcourt was doing a signing, he came and explained his own book to him for nearly an hour. You can just imagine how Delcourt . . . And he's also got that nervous tic with his fists, you always feel he's about to smash your face in."

"I didn't notice," says Yves.

YVES AND ANNA

. . .

*A*NNA WILL BE FORTY TOMORROW. For the first time in
years, she has not planned a party. She could not imagine
celebrating her birthday without Yves, and, in her indecision, she
waited until it was too late to send out invitations.

She is walking along the street, in a hurry. She is meeting
Yves and he has promised her a present. Not long after they
met, he gave her a ring, a silver one, which swivels and opens
like an oyster to reveal its secret, a yellow diamond nestled in
golden mother-of-pearl. But this piece of jewelry has stayed in
the bottom of a drawer, under a silk scarf.

Of course Yves is already at the café, he is reading the paper, in
no rush. Anna hates being waited for impatiently, she hates being
a prisoner to someone else's attachment. She wants something that
does not exist: a lover who adores her, but is utterly indifferent.

She has hardly sat down opposite him before he hands her
a small package wrapped in red crepe paper. She opens it, it

contains five books, all identical. They are small, ivory-colored, about sixty pages long.

She looks up again. Almost frightened.

"Don't worry," says Yves. "Only ten copies were made. You have half the edition there."

"Thank you," says Anna. "Can I read it now?"

"I hope you will," Yves replies. "It's not very long."

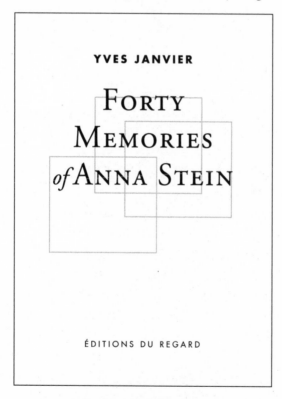

YVES JANVIER

FORTY
MEMORIES
of ANNA STEIN

ÉDITIONS DU REGARD

Where do our memories file themselves away? Broca proved that the left hemisphere controls speech, Penfield maintains that the temporal lobes house memory. So an arrangement of neurons, a chemistry within the brain stocks the images, sounds, and smells that I call memories of you. Why is it my hands themselves hold the memory of your skin?

I want forty memories of you, Anna. For the reason you can guess. Forty is a lot, think of Ali Baba's thieves. And forty is too few: it means resigning myself to never retracing a gesture you make, one so specific to you, so intimate; not describing the sight of a street with your silhouette outlined against it; not referring to something you said even though it touched me; it means abandoning certain characteristics on the grounds that I have already put them in writing, somewhere else.

Describing too precisely is pointless, and I am conscious of the risk I run, which is platitude. And yet I run it, for memory itself runs a greater risk and that is forgetting, given that forgetting is merely the natural fate of all memory. But what I know above all else is that each of these memories is here, set down in words in order to accomplish the impossible: never to lose you.

ONE

It's a very vague recollection, a haze of a memory. You're talking, standing in the middle of the huge foyer in an apartment on the Left Bank. I say "you," but that's absurd because I don't yet know that you are you. The people who will play a part in our lives are always strangers the day before we meet them, and writing it has less to do with naïveté than wonderment.

You're talking about incest and rape. Your eyes reveal a rare vivaciousness, your voice has a penetrating lilting quality, your diction is precise, confident, I detect an urgency in your quick-fire delivery that is not related to the subject but to the way you are. The clothes you're wearing seem to float over you. Your hair skims your shoulders. I don't look at you much, only because I so desperately want to look at you. I don't want my eagerness to betray my growing desire, I don't want my too obvious attention to embarrass you. Even now, I regret those first minutes when I didn't allow myself to grasp you more fully, see you more clearly.

TWO

You may remember this better than me. We're having *tagliatelle al pesto ligure* for dinner in that Italian restaurant on the rue Mazarine, surrounded by people I know nothing about. We don't know each other, I'm drawn to you, aroused by you. If you had not followed us there for dinner, I would have gone home.

We're talking about the Holocaust, the camps, Belzec, and it's more than I can take, I can't hide the tears in my eyes; later you will tell me you found that moving. You suddenly say these words: "my husband, my children." I think: obviously. A woman like you couldn't not have ties. The distress I feel when you indicate that nothing is possible lays me bare, it tells me how lonely I've always been, without you. A self-evident fact comes to light: I'm no longer in any doubt that you are a woman for me.

You're the one who will use the word "thunderbolt." But later, in a profile published in the periodical *Quinzaine*, when the journalist asks me the ten key dates in my life, my last milestone will be: "September this year. *Struck by a thunderbolt.*"

THREE

Let's say this right away, there will be no chronology, no true logic, and definitely no hierarchy. The last memory described will simply be the last. It will just be the face of a die showing when it has stopped rolling, because every die thrown eventually stops rolling. As far as this third memory is concerned, it isn't in its rightful place, but who cares.

It's an autumn evening, you drop by my apartment toward the end of the afternoon, and bring some pastries for the three of us, because my daughter is with me: an apple tart, a pear tart, and a custard tart. You have split the three pastries and you're eating the filling, leaving the crust and bottom. I point out to my daughter that she mustn't behave like that if she's invited to someone's house. You burst out laughing: you've just realized that you've "made yourself at home."

You're no longer visiting.

FOUR

We're naked in bed, lying beneath the sheets. You're listing things you like: going under bridges, looking down over open countryside, scouring your mind to find the exact word for something, feeling the men you love looking at you . . . You haven't mentioned "buying clothes." I remind you of this one; you're amazed not to have thought of it. I wanted to remember everything: you also like to have a very soft light on when you sleep alone at night, old churches, being wanted and being taken, and quattrocento art. In no particular order.

FIVE

You're asleep. You're lying on your back with your knees together, legs bent and feet splayed. The whole arrangement forms a very stable pyramid that I can't push over. There's a draft under the duvet and it's not warming up. No one can sleep in that position. And yet you're asleep, fast asleep, no chance of getting you to move an inch. The following morning you won't believe me, obviously.

SIX

It's a telephone conversation. We will have a thousand of them, and that's not much of an exaggeration. This one is about the five hundredth.

The train is cutting across the Moran region, I'm drinking coffee in the restaurant car, watching the undulating fields scud past. I hear you say: "I was thinking, for our wedding I'll wear a red dress." I *will* wear, not I *would*, I can feel the difference. If you're picturing your clothes then it's really serious. For the next ten minutes we talk about the ceremony, the venue, the guests, the musicians, I know you're joking, I also know that you're enjoying the game, that it gives you a right to project us into the taboo that a union between us would represent.

From time to time, the train passes a village. I spot a church tower, there is probably also a register office, but almost certainly no synagogue.

SEVEN

One more round on the carousel at the Jardin des Plantes and your little girl climbs down from the wooden horse. Lea hasn't succeeded in hooking the pink pompom, despite the best efforts of the woman in the booth: a redheaded child—in a better position and more competitive—managed to get it before her every time. We sit at a table by the refreshment stand, two coffees, one hot chocolate. Lea has forgotten her scooter and you have to go and get it, so she and I are left facing each other, watching each other in silence, me rather cautiously looking down, she mischievously peering up.

It's the first time we've met properly. I think she looks like you, despite her blond hair and blue eyes. You come back over, and we head toward the largest conservatory. All of a sudden, Lea sneaks in between the two of us. She takes your hand and then, by surprise, mine, and starts swinging between us. With that one gesture, your little girl is giving me permission to exist, and her tiny hand is offering me a position that it alone has any right to grant.

We go down the steps into the conservatory, with Lea between us skipping and laughing. Thanks to her, we are side by side for the first time.

EIGHT

I heard the water running, secretly opened the door to the bathroom, and now I'm watching you. You're naked, taking a shower. Mind you, one of your friends has given you a piece of unfaithful woman's advice: "Never smell of soap when you go home in the evening." Under the circumstances, it's difficult to do without it, but at least let's make sure it's the same soap as usual. I have bought myself some. You arch your back, avoiding getting your hair wet so there is no moisture on it to give you away. Your buttock shadows into a dimple I have never seen before, your smooth skin forms goose bumps in the cold, your nipples are still erect.

You will tell me, later, that you like very hot showers, or very cold ones, showers that produce a burning sensation. The window behind you looks out over the city, its lights coming on as night falls. You're not aware of me watching you; soon you will turn, will be surprised, and, delighted, you will smile at me.

NINE

We're walking down the hill on the rue du Chevalier de la Barre (1743–1760). I have my arm around your waist and you've allowed me to, even though Paris may be full of all these "people you know," which means that from the Place de la Concorde to the Marais I'm not allowed to kiss you. But, in the middle of the street, you take my hand and put it on your ass, spontaneous and provocative in equal measures. My hand seems happy with the arrangement, and so does your ass. I immediately want you. One day you will formulate a sentence referring to, if I remember, "the role played by desire in the corpus of our relationship," and I will smile. For now, I like feeling your buttocks moving beneath my hand.

TEN

It's just a desk, straight lines, a modern feel dating from the sixties. There it is, abandoned on the sidewalk on the rue des Abbesses. You really like it, so do I. You love hunting around for antiques, I thought you would. You decide to take it and go to get your car; we have some trouble putting it into the trunk. You're planning to paint the steel feet red. Or black. I agree. Where will it live? With you, in Paris or Burgundy, or, one day, with us? That last option gets my vote. Either way, it's our first piece of furniture. Wherever it lives its desk life, it will bring you back to memories of us.

ELEVEN

I also have memories of you that don't include you, memories of the two of us that you won't know about at all. Where you are such a strong presence in me that your absence is almost imperceptible. It's the imprint of you on the sand of me, the silent melody that your existence leaves in me. In one of these memories, I'm walking along the cloisters of an abbey, sheltered from the rain by a Roman vaulted ceiling. I sit down on some stone stairs, surrounded by the sound of footsteps, voices, children calling. All I can think of is you. The day before, I held you in my arms for the first time, and you've invaded me already. Sentences about you come to me, and I write them down, with no clear intention yet. Legend would have it that a piece of shrapnel lodged in Shostakovich's brain meant that, if he tilted his head a particular way, he could hear unknown pieces of music. You are my Shostakovich's shrapnel. *Shostakovich's Shrapnel* would make a good title for a novel. Life is full of good titles for novels.

TWELVE

I know the exact place. I could trace the outline of your feet and mine with white chalk, the way a forensic scientist draws a line around the body at a crime scene, or a dance teacher makes diagrams of basic dance positions. It's here, in the kitchen, between the refrigerator and the wooden table. You're in my apartment for the first time, you're walking ahead of me and you suddenly stop. It's so obvious that I should take you in my arms. Besides, I am walking so close behind you that, if I don't, I'll run into you. I put my arms around you, my chest touches your back, my mouth reaches for the back of your neck, you turn in my arms and we kiss.

One day, I'll draw those marks on the floor tiles. They'll prove to you that you're not a mermaid, because mermaids don't have feet.

THIRTEEN

You're succumbing to tiredness, your breathing's getting quieter, your eyes closing in the warm bed. You suddenly start talking about tobacco pouches. What you're saying is incoherent, but even so I try to make some sense of it (I know the people close to you who do have tobacco tins); I've forgotten what I said to you, but you use the words "tin" and "red paper," your words growing less distinct. I haven't grasped that you're already asleep, haven't yet discovered that, of all the threads connecting you to the conscious world, speech is the most enduring, the one you consent to relinquish only after you have sunk into sleep.

FOURTEEN

Without thinking what you're doing, and not even aware you're doing it, I think, you put your hand firmly against my temple and force my head down onto the sheet. Either way, it's clear that you want to use me to your own ends. I'm surprised at first, so surprised that my neck—which is as amazed as the rest of me—resists for a moment before giving in to your invitation.

Then I laugh, and so do you, about the intimacy between our bodies over which we have no control.

FIFTEEN

You drag me into a clothing store, opposite the pretty Enfants-Rouges market on the rue de Bretagne. It's the first time. I've not yet gauged how important jewelry and fabrics are to you. You go into the boutique with all the confidence and simplicity of a regular, fingering dresses and tops, asking my opinion, which I give. The prices seem high but I'm far from informed: in the months to come, I will learn a lot. You slip into a fitting room to try on a denim dress, through the gap in the white canvas drapes I glimpse your hips and red lace panties. I don't know you well enough yet to risk popping my head in and gazing at you almost naked. But just for the time it takes you to try on a dress, I like being the man beside you in life: I think the hat fits me pretty well.

SIXTEEN

The telephone rings, and it's you. Your breasts are "enormous," that's the word you use, because you're pregnant, you're in absolutely no doubt: "I know my body," you say, unequivocally. I'm at Roissy airport, about to board for Berlin, and, given that I believe in this pregnancy and feel no shred of fear at the prospect, I see something clearly: I want a life with you. You hang up and there I am, for a few hours, the potential father of a little Sarah or a little, now what would it be, Jude?

And, in spite of the inevitable drama, the tears to come and the heartache, do you know what? I'm happy.

SEVENTEEN

"Do you know what?" That's *your* phrase. A relic from adolescence that you haven't shaken off, a linguistic weakness I find touching. What do you use it for, what role does it play in the way you speak? Is it a pause you allow yourself to give you a better chance to formulate an idea that comes to you? I take the question seriously every time, I answer no, quietly, which is my own discreet way of saying how interested I am in you, and how much I care too.

EIGHTEEN

It's already dark on the rue de Grenelle, you're back with your children. But, so that I don't have to leave you quite yet, I'm following the three of you around Monoprix, with no valid excuse.

Karl and Lea are energetically maneuvering between the aisles with their mini shopping carts decked out with flags. On your instructions, they pile up cornflakes, sugar, yogurts . . . For their sakes, you transform the chore of shopping into an exciting game, a treasure hunt. I briefly interpret this frenzy as your fear that life might stop being a party, as if you owed it—to yourself and your children—to be a fairy.

A fragile side of you emerges from this feverish activity as an attentive wife and mother, and I find it touching, it bowls me over. I restrain my mounting urge to take the kindly sorceress in my arms, and protect her from the demons of routine and boredom.

NINETEEN

You think you know how to go about catching me. You do. But how can I describe my desire, the way my hands thirst for your skin, my lips for yours? There's no point describing what we do, choosing one thing among a thousand. That's what I'm doing here.

Our nakedness, side by side. I like looking at you naked, you like me looking at you. You're lying on your stomach, desirable, offered up, but a man's body doesn't always obey him so readily; and you may deny it, but that is something you definitely regret.

I am sitting on the bed looking at your nakedness, when your buttocks turn and rise up toward me, their every curve wanting to arouse me, their soft, soft skin intended just for me. You smile, and this gesture gets the better of me, I'm gripped by desire, you are mine and I take you.

TWENTY

It's very late, you have to go: your husband is on duty, the children with their grandparents, but your guilt won't let you sleep at my apartment, it persuades you to go home.

It's winter, the weather's cold. As usual, I walk you to your car, expecting to accompany you to your neighborhood and come back by taxi afterward. It's a ritual we have, a way of stealing another half hour from the time we don't have together. We're getting close to the Renault, I see you stop dead in your tracks. There's a man sitting in the driver's seat, sound asleep. You're petrified, unable to make a single move. I knock on the window, in vain, I open the door, pat the man on the shoulder gently, then more insistently. He wakes, with some difficulty, and I ask him, not unkindly, to get out of the car.

This homeless person is young, probably a foreigner, Polish, Russian . . . he's embarrassed, mutters a few words of apology, he hauls himself out of the vehicle, still groggy with sleep, and walks off into the night. He's left his backpack on the passenger seat,

I run after him to give it back. You're still standing on the sidewalk, shocked, unable to get into the car that's been desecrated by an intruder. You feel sick, you're still shaking. "I'll drive, if you like," I suggest. You agree, you know I'm happy to shoulder the role of a man you can depend on. You've just discovered a facet of me you didn't know, and it seems to amaze you.

We drive to your apartment, you seem flattened by exhaustion. You say, "You're nice," and it's not meant as a reproach, even though you hate people being "nice." I shake my head but you insist: "Yes, you are, you're nice. You were very nice to that man. You're not frightened of people, you're not frightened of approaching them." You suddenly like the fact that I can be nice. From now on, it's no longer just a sign of weakness to you.

TWENTY-ONE

Your perfume: *Eau de lierre*. A "nose" would define it like this: the head notes are very green with a vegetal elegance, until the ivy discreetly gives way and eclipses itself before tones of stone and dry wood. It could be a fragrance worn by an effete man, but on your skin the warm musks and spices win over. We're already a long way from our animal state, and when I close my eyes, I can't conjure up that smell as well as I can the image of your face. It will always be the color of the back of your neck where I completely lose myself, and, if I lose you, it will be the smell of my nostalgia.

TWENTY-TWO

It's an evening in December, the car is pulling away from the neon lights on the Place Clichy and easing as best it can onto the busy Boulevard des Batignolles. You're off to pick up your children.

I don't know how we've ended up talking about death, but you suddenly say: "If I had a terminal illness, a cancer, I don't think I'd have any hesitation, I'd come and live with you." Perhaps it's out of modesty, but I quote Woody Allen: "Life is a terminal illness." But you're already parking, and your words are still worrying away at me.

I measure the scope of your declaration. It's not the emergency itself you're talking about here, but the requirement for truthfulness that emergencies demand of us. All at once, I grasp something else, between the lines: that, with me, you would leave the serenity of an illusory eternity where your days are not counted, for an unreliable world in which they are. Illness would finally launch you into that world where time actually passes. I understand what it is that I give you, it's being afraid.

TWENTY-THREE

A café outside the Scuola Musica, in winter. You've left me to look after Lea, or maybe it's Lea who's keeping an eye on me. At first she wants to play a board game with kings and queens, then, because she gets bored with it or because she wants to show me different games, picture dominoes. She has hot chocolate, I have coffee, as usual: I like feeling she and I have our own habits. She stirs the froth with her spoon, I make sure she doesn't spill any. You've taken Karl to his music theory lesson, but you come right back.

To Lea, I'm Yves, mommy's friend who sometimes has a suitcase because he's going a long way away. I don't know what makes you think of this question but you ask: "Who's the wolf?" "Me!" Lea replies artlessly. Then, very pleased with herself, she adds: "Mommy is mommy wolf and Yves is daddy wolf." You're embarrassed but also upset, you correct her, bringing the real daddy back into the equation.

I can still picture Lea, with that impish look you sometimes have, bursting out laughing.

TWENTY-FOUR

It's a memory of memories. You leading me through your apartment, to your bedroom. You go to a closet and take out some cardboard boxes. Photographs, lots of them. Then you take me to the kitchen so you can show them to me properly.

It's your life.

You with your little boy, under a Christmas tree. Your daughter running across a garden I don't recognize, another one of her, with your husband. You hesitate for a moment, then show me still more photos, your wedding I think, though I'm not sure. I'm launched into your world, submerged by a wave of snapshots of your life before, where I don't belong. I understand what you're doing, what it means, the desire for intimacy that it presupposes, but I'm slowly drowning in this tide of pictures. You don't notice, but imperceptibly I take a step back, to avoid suffocating. You rummage through the box some more. One by one, you take out pictures of yourself, set them to one side, give them to me.

I know who took them, who you're smiling at, but all of a sudden that doesn't matter. It's you that you're giving to me. I accept the gift.

TWENTY-FIVE

You've run to get here, late, to this restaurant by the flea market in Saint-Ouen which, over the last few weeks, has become our Monday meeting place. You sit down opposite me, I can tell from the haphazard way you're moving that something's going on. You're putting on a sort of performance, saying you're sick, some infection you can't pin down, later you go on to call yourself a "stupid bitch," not a word you normally use. You don't want to meet my eye, you don't feel any love for me anymore, your desire has evaporated. You're not all anger, but I'm in pieces.

A gaping hole opens before me. I picture myself permanently and irrevocably indebted to you, and yours. You know how the story ends, which is almost laughable, so this memory is only there to describe that moment, that feeling of vertigo, the capsizing, when our relationship switched from happy and lighthearted to ugly and messy. A stain, that's the word that comes to mind at the time, but I don't say it for fear it could be so accurate that it spatters onto us. But it keeps coming back to me, filling my whole head, stopping me from speaking, when I really should speak.

TWENTY-SIX

We're in the car heading for Paris, I'm driving. My hand has eased between your bare legs, where it feels happy. A few minutes ago you were still wearing jeans. At a service station, where you thought I wouldn't dare stop, you swapped them for a dress. My stroking becomes more focused, my right hand growing adventurous while my left drives attentively. Your thighs open for my fingers, they creep still farther up and start having fun. I'm playing with your desire in the same way that you're playing with mine. What we're doing is more spontaneous than provocative, more to do with amazement than perversity. Your whole body smiles at mine, happily.

TWENTY-SEVEN

We're in the toy department of Bon Marché. You're looking for a princess dress for Lea and a cowboy outfit for Karl. You move away a few feet, and I watch you surrounded by Barbie dolls, Playmobil garages, and boxes of Legos. I follow you through the aisles: undecided, you call the children's father for advice, then, almost before you've hung up, you want my opinion. I give it, amazed that you see me as such an intimate stranger. You're leaving the door to your life ajar for me, while I stray through the cuddly toys, gazing at them tenderly with a bitter-sweet taste in my mouth.

TWENTY-EIGHT

"Take care of yourself." Those are the words you'll leave with. Really leave. We're standing next to the car, opposite the Gare de l'Est rail station, it's December, a beautiful day.

Only minutes earlier, you spoke the few sentences which make it impossible for us to stay together with the same happy-go-lucky feeling as before, sentences that mean I have to say I'm going. Not leaving now would mean losing you, and that's why I'm leaving, to keep intact the possibility of coming back to you.

"Take care of yourself." The tender, tender words a father says to his son before he goes away, to die. They tell me you will no longer be there to watch over me, but have you ever watched over me? You head for your Renault, turn back to face me. Then, after briefly catching my eye, your body suddenly rebels, throws itself at me, holds me tightly. For a fleeting moment, I fill myself with its smell, its warmth, then you resist and break away from me, for real. The wind carries off your sweet perfume, by the time the car starts up and drives off, there's nothing of you left, I walk mechanically toward the bus that will take me home.

I cross the street on autopilot, watching out for the number 31 bus speeding past, I have no desire to die, the pain makes me feel unbelievably alive.

TWENTY-NINE

This twenty-ninth memory is of a short night spent writing feverishly. Remember: a little iron box, stolen because you hid it in your handbag. I gave it to you four days after we met. It held "Twenty-six tiny moments between us," printed on pieces of paper the size of a Métro ticket. One of them said:

> *I've done the math, we've seen each other*
> *Three times, it's almost unbelievable.*
> *Do you think you can dream something like this?*
> *That none of it is real?*

THIRTY

They've sold two and a half million of your Renault Twingo cars, a million of them in and around Paris, and almost one in three is black (I've checked). It's in this virtually invisible model that we're driving around the Place de la Concorde. It's dark and raining, the windows are opaque with condensation. I try to kiss your neck. You protest sharply. "I know everyone around here."

THIRTY-ONE

It's a photocopy of an insurance statement that I've lovingly kept. You slammed on your brakes on the rue Pouchet in the Seventeenth Arrondissement, opposite the passage Berzélius, and the car behind ran into yours. On the back of the statement, where it says "Circumstances of the Accident," still shaken by the event, you wrote: "My vehicle (A) must of knocked . . ."

You show it to me later, laughing at your slipup, your mistake. Sometimes, quite often actually, I read that statement, and it immediately makes me smile. You who always do the right thing, who's always so precise in her choice of words, you easily get swamped by the contingencies of daily life. What that statement, that "must of," reveals is a trace of you rubbing up against the world.

THIRTY-TWO

You're having a bath (a very hot one) in my apartment. I sit down beside you on the wooden step and slip my right hand into the water, up to the elbow, it comes to rest on you. It's an instinctive move, I have so little control over what I do when I'm with you. Talking alone takes such a lot of my concentration. My fingers glide over your breasts, your hips, stroke your stomach, move down between your legs. I kiss you and your lips open slightly, your tongue plays with mine, you close your eyes. My middle finger is intrepid but respectful, pushing gently into your pussy and between your buttocks. I fill myself with the moment, already aware that this sensual experience will only ever be a sensory memory, will never be captured by words trying to define it.

THIRTY-THREE

A text message makes my cell phone vibrate. I look at the time, and know that you've typed it at Kennedy Airport, where you're about to take flight AF 544 to Paris–Charles de Gaulle. In a moment of panic before getting onto the Boeing, you write: "if anythg happens 2 me, my 2008 notebks r 4 u." Still a respect for punctuation. I can't help smiling and this is the reply you get: "U r crazy. But I want somethg 2 happen 2 u."

In one of Virginia Woolf's novels, a woman dies in an accident, a suicide perhaps? She bequeaths her personal diary to her husband. In it he discovers the existence of another man, a more and more prevalent presence as he reads on. He sets out to find this other man and, particularly, the other man's wife.

If you died, how would I dare claim those notebooks? I can't imagine it and yet I would do it. What you're offering me is the subject of a play: one man knocks at the door of another man who is in mourning. They don't know each other. The first simply says: "I've come to ask for your wife's notebooks, the ones she's written over the last year. We were in love. She left them to me."

THIRTY-FOUR

The Porte de la Chapelle one Friday afternoon, at nearly four o'clock. I get into your little car and we head for your children's school, you're late, of course.

All these journeys—how many of them were there, twenty, thirty?—get confused in my memory like a multicolored mosaic. Over all those months, we saw blue skies and gray ones, driving rain and summer sun. You wore jeans, black dresses, white skirts, woolen sweaters, floaty blouses, you were too hot and you were very cold. But the rue Saint-Martin was always the same, noisy and stagnant with traffic, inside your black Renault, laden with files and papers. Our conversations covered everything and nothing.

One hour. Every Friday. I smile.

THIRTY-FIVE

Florence. I'm there for a reading and have succeeded in taking you with me. From among all the postcard memories, and other more intimate ones, I've chosen a dinner we had in a chic restaurant with working-class decor, as so many of them in that city are.

We're sitting side by side and you're talking to Luciana, the young blond woman opposite you. From time to time I turn toward you and Luciana smiles, touched by my little look which means I'm watching over you. She recognizes in it the look of attentive kindness her husband gives her when his banking job means he has to take her along to dinners with clients, and he's worried she's getting bored. Now it's your turn to laugh, and because there is a growing friendship between you, you mention your husband and children, that other life I don't belong to, and you take my hand, in a spontaneous gesture that expresses your love and your uncertainties.

THIRTY-SIX

It's a Saturday in late October: I'm walking through the Père-Lachaise cemetery where tourists wander among the graves, getting lost down its pathways. I go slowly in the direction of the crematorium.

Hugues Léger's body is being burned beneath the zinc cupola. I write that sentence in all its extraordinary violence. I can picture you, mute and petrified, confronted with this, with Hugues's second, definitive disappearance. I came so that I could be there by your side, without asking whether I could. I took the initiative, it seemed the right thing to do. I sit down on a bench, send you a text, and wait.

For reasons that still escape me, now that Hugues Léger is no more, I feel a closeness to him that has nothing morbid about it: I'm not fascinated by death, but his suicide has affected me. I would even go so far as to say, without feeling presumptuous, that it overwhelms me. I know how different we were, but can now see our similarities. Is the best day of my life already behind me too?

It's as I sit on that bench that I realize with genuine sadness that I let a friendship—between men, between writers—pass me by, and that you would have liked it if we'd become friends.

You don't seem to figure in this memory, and yet it's for you, and you alone, that I'm here, on this bench.

THIRTY-SEVEN

You're asleep, I'm not. You fell asleep in my arms without completely leaving me but now you really are fast asleep, already.

Propped on one elbow with my head resting on my hand, I watch you. You snore almost imperceptibly. Your eyes are closed, your mouth half open, and your lips sketch that very soft, very rare smile—and this is not a cliché—that belongs to you alone. You're beautiful, free. Thoughts come to me: What are you dreaming about? Where are you at that moment? Who are you that I'm so afraid of losing you, why do I so want you to be mine, why am I sure you'll never be completely mine?

I'm ashamed of this longing for ownership that I can't quite put my finger on. It reveals my share of the terror that a woman's freedom to desire arouses in men. I don't like the dumb beast in me awakened by the fear that one day you'll no longer desire me. I wish I could be serene, feel no more doubt.

I lie on my back, I can't get to sleep.

THIRTY-EIGHT

Stay a couple more minutes, you say. We had said goodbye for the last time, yet again. But then my cell phone rang and it was you, we talked, possibly just to hear each other's voices one last time. I was about to hang up: "Stay a couple more minutes." It's okay, I stay a couple more minutes. I don't say anything and neither do you, I can just hear your breathing, from time to time. Your breathing is more devastating than any words you could have said. Time passes, I walk up the street, reach my building and go in, but I stay in the lobby, leaning against the wall. We stay like that in silence, for a long time. I'm sure that, like me, you're filling yourself up with this shared silence, in anticipation of a much longer one to come, one we won't be sharing anymore.

THIRTY-NINE

Of course, this little book is coming to an end and I'm regretting it already. I promised myself I would be strict, but just remember: a text telling me you're going to do four things (the first was to have your ears pierced); me almost like a teenager the first (and only) time I met your parents; your little boy deciding to hit me by way of a greeting at Luc's concert; you, at the wheel of your car, on the first day, struggling to fasten your seat belt and, when I try to help, uttering a polysemic "Oh, are you getting involved?"; you at your house, wearing a black dress and a doubly secret ring; your voice reading Dorothy Parker to me on the banks of the Seine; your hand dragging me into the corner of the kitchen where the neighbors can't see us; you kissed avidly under a porch in the Jardin des Batignolles; and you, again, always you, coming down the stairs of a library where I'm doing a reading of one of my books, discovering my public persona, feeling thrilled and in love.

FORTY

My die has finally come to rest on this surface. I promised a lack of logic and yet there has been some: this last memory is imaginary, it happens at some time in the near future as I write to you now. I don't know where we've arranged to meet, I don't know if we've even really split up, I only know the date, around January 10.

I look at you and say: "I have a present for you. For your fortieth birthday." I produce this tiny book. You read the title, leaf through it for a moment. You may be moved, perhaps very moved. I know what you want more than anything: for me to work. This is a piece of work, and you can tell. You know that every sentence was written and rewritten, not just for you but for everyone else too, you sense that what you have in your hand is the raw material for another piece, a longer one, still to come. But, in spite of everything, this is a book, a book that really was written for you.

I won't add, "I wish it had been longer," because that's not true, or "I wish I'd had more time," because I did have time, almost too much. I wish I could have written it in a week, been caught up in writing it and not in the upheavals of our relationship. That is not how it happened, I wasn't granted that whole week.

Because I myself am moved, disarmed, I might quite easily whisper an "I love you," already regretting that sometimes that's all I can think to say to you.

And if you can read one more sentence, and these few words, then a real declaration could never bring a real book to a conclusion.

YVES AND ANNA

. . .

YVES LETS ANNA READ *Forty Memories of Anna Stein,* and leafs through his newspaper, trying to take an interest in articles. She has not looked up at him once, has read the book straight through, in twenty minutes.

Anna puts the book down.

"Thank you," she says again.

THOMAS AND LOUISE

. . .

IT IS THE LAST SUNDAY IN FEBRUARY. Thomas has taken Louise, Judith, and Maud to the races in Vincennes. They have never seen trotting races, or any sort of horse racing, period. Louise could not make up her mind because it was drizzling, it was windy, it was cold, but she wanted to please Thomas. They are in the grandstand, to the west of the track.

"The second race will start in two minutes" is called out over the loudspeakers.

"I haven't been for years. When I was ten, I used to come with my grandfather, he always bet on the second and fourth races, very small stakes."

"Could we bet too?" Judith asks.

Thomas is in favor, but as he turns to Louise, she scowls.

"Absolutely not," she says. "I know all about these places. They launder dirty money."

"How does money get dirty, mom?" Maud asks.

"Just for one race," Thomas persists. "Coming here and not betting really would be a shame."

"Please yourself," Louise sighs. "But I'm not putting one centime of my money into this."

"Great," says Thomas. "Come on, girls, we're having a go at it."

The betting booths are close by. They are back in a flash, the girls holding slips in their hands.

"I backed Cabbage Patch Hurricane to win, mom," cries Judith. "He was sixty-seven to one!"

"And I backed Oscars Night to place," adds Maud. "At thirty-eight to one!"

The girls' excitement raises a smile from Louise.

"They really are a dead loss, the pair of them," Thomas says apologetically, "but the girls liked their names so much. They spent ten euros each. Is that okay? It's pretty reasonable."

"Twenty euros in all? It's far too much, Thomas. It's ridiculous."

"The second race will start in one minute," says the announcer.

"The horses are on the track over there," Thomas explains. "They're going to line up in front of us for the start, and when the pistol's fired, they'll set off at top speed, turn over there to the east and come back in front of us for the finish."

"Which one is Cabbage Patch Hurricane?" Judith asks.

"He's number 12, over there. With the purple hat."

The little girls are startled by the *bang* of the starting gun, then they giggle at their jumpiness and start screaming the names of their respective horses. Thomas roars with laughter, Louise is embarrassed.

"Not so much noise, girls, you're disturbing other people."

The geldings are already tackling the sweeping turn. Judging by the commentary, Judith's horse is in quite a good position.

The favorite, Piet van Dresde, has slightly grazed his pastern and is not at his best. His rival, Orus de Bruxelles, is finding the heavy going difficult. The others are giving a mediocre performance. When the horses cross the finish line, the commentator announces: "First: number 12, Cabbage Patch Hurricane. Second: number 10, Oscars Night. Third: number 3, Piet van Dresde."

"Did they win?" Louise asks, astonished.

Thomas is no less surprised.

"I can't believe it. Yes, your daughters have won. And both of them, too."

Judith and Maud jump and dance for joy, jigging in a circle and singing, "We won, we won!"

"Did they back Hurricane to win?" a tall man asks with a note of astonishment as he tears up his own betting slip. "That bag of bones? Some people have all the luck."

"Hu-rri-cane! Hu-rri-cane!" the girls chant.

"Stop! Calm down, girls. But . . . Thomas . . . how much have they won?"

"It's incredible. Almost a thousand euros between them."

"A thou-sand! A thou-sand! A thou-sand!"

"Quiet!" Louise barks furiously. "Come on, we're going home."

"But, mommy, can't we bet again?" Judith asks.

"No, I said we're going home. Do you hear me?"

"Please, mommy," Maud wheedles. "Thomas said we could bet again on the fourth race."

"I said no. And it's me who decides, not Thomas. Okay?"

Louise snatches her daughters by the hand and drags them down from the grandstand in spite of their protestations. Thomas does not argue. He goes to collect the winnings and meets them back at the car, where they are already sitting in their seats. Louise is at the wheel, silent; the engine is running and the girls are chirping away in the back. Thomas produces a roll of bills.

"What shall we do with this honestly won money?"

Louise does not reply. She drives off and slips onto the belt-way, staring at the road ahead, stony-faced.

"Can you explain, Louise? What's going on? I thought the whole thing was funny."

"You don't understand anything. No, Thomas, it's not funny. The girls are so overexcited, you might as well have given them cocaine."

"Cocaine?"

"That's exactly right. Gambling's addictive, didn't you know that? And I don't even recognize my own daughters. I'm angry with you."

"I'm really sorry."

"Sorry . . . Well, it's too late. I know plenty of people who blow everything in casinos, even their pension. Do you really want to know? My own mother, that's who. My mother. In Enghien. And even now she goes whenever she can. I can't tell you the memories this brings back."

"You should have told me . . ."

"I didn't want to go to Vincennes, but you insisted. There. You won."

They sit in silence. For a long time. The traffic moves slug-gishly. In the back, the girls have stopped talking. Thomas turns around: they are asleep, exhausted. The dashboard gives off a long beeping sound.

"Damn. I've run out of gas," Louise says irritably. "And I don't have my credit card."

"I have some cash," Thomas whispers. "Quite a lot, even."

She does not answer. He looks sideways at her. Louise's lips sketch a smile, which grows wider. Gradually they succumb to hysterical laughter, the car zigzags slightly. The girls do not wake.

STAN

. . .

$\mathcal{L}$OOKING OUT OF A HOTEL ROOM WINDOW, Stan watches the wintry night fall over Lisbon.

A long line of waiting taxis coils around Rossio Square, sheltered by plane trees. The evening shower has stopped, the pedestrians are no longer a ballet of black umbrellas. The next fare is a hefty woman weighed down with bags. She huffs and puffs, railing against the wind and the rain, everything is making her life difficult, her shopping, her soaked raincoat, her own weight. She is bound to go by some respectable name, Senhora Costa perhaps, yes, that's it, Senhora Manuela Costa. She is in a hurry to get home so she can put it all away in closets before Senhor Costa comes home, and she is probably persuading herself that, as she has so much to carry, a taxi isn't an unreasonable expense after all. She smiles and tells herself life is sometimes as beautiful as a large department store.

Behind Stan, under the sheets, a woman lies sleeping, her cheek crushed on the pillow. In this unconscious state, the vague resemblance to Vermeer's *Girl with a Pearl Earring* that Stan managed to grant her evaporates altogether. The sleeper's name is Marianne Laurent, she is married, admits to being thirty-five, laughs for no reason, and works in Lyon, at the Edouard Herriot Hospital, in Bongrand's department, where she operates on corneas, which explains why she was at the sixth congress of the European Association for Vision and Eye Research. Stan now also knows that she has had work on her lips and breasts, has a pronounced predisposition to oral sex and a tendency to give short squealing sounds. They drank port together, too much of it, at the hotel bar. She was the one who dragged him to her room, her mind made up; he let her take the initiative before inverting the roles with a physical fury he did not know he was capable of.

Stan rests his forehead against the windowpane, his skin hoping to feel a bite of cold. Each taxi completes the same slow revolution around the fountain and Dom Pedro IV's column. Stan has time to look at each driver's face, to pick out the one who wears an ugly gray wool cardigan whatever the weather, the one who prefers a short-sleeved shirt to a polo shirt. They each have their own way of getting the customer inside. One turns around with a genuine smile, another waits for instructions, grumbling and keeping his eyes pinned on the steering wheel. If a driver has to put bags in the trunk, the routine procedure reveals everything about him, his sciatica, his filthy mood, his habits. Stan can give him a whole life, a wife, a mistress, one, two, or three children, he pictures the dog, a poodle or a bulldog, snoozing on the passenger seat.

Marianne Laurent snores artlessly, her mouth open. Anna

used to say that for men, and sometimes for women, the sexual act could be—and this was her word—"vacuous." Stan has to face the facts. He gave in to this woman's moves, to the point of succumbing to his own body's voracious appetites, and he took her without tenderness or love, striving for annihilation in a state of appalling loneliness. He closes his eyes. He would like to forget himself again in the passionate eagerness of those unfamiliar lips, lose himself one last time in that pliant, yearning flesh.

But the taxis keep circling the square and Stan is drawn into their slow spiral, which suddenly takes his thoughts back to Anna, to the grim thought of Anna's naked body beneath someone else's, and the image that looms in his mind pulverizes him.

THOMAS AND LOUISE

. . .

I remember when rock was young,
Me and Suzie had so much fun,
Holding hands and skimming stones,
Had an old gold Chevy and a place of my own,
But the biggest kick I ever got
Was doing a thing called the Crocodile Rock

Elton John and Bernie Taupin's song dates back to the sixties, but the Farfisa organ and its honky-tonk have not aged that much. Louise has danced to "Crocodile Rock" so many times that it reminds her of being thirteen as readily as it does of being thirty. Later, she does not yet know this, it will remind her of being forty. After a Radiohead song, Thomas was out of breath and he abandoned Louise for a stool by the bar. She is spinning in some tall blond guy's arms, her skirt twirling up. Louise has had a bit to drink.

The tall blond man is called Boris, and Thomas has gathered the fact—because the guy was going to great lengths to make it known—that he has a talk show on a cable channel. He is a pretty good-looking boy, the sporty type, with a very newscaster haircut, probably the best catch at this party. He is taking a very close interest in Louise. Earlier, when they were chatting, Boris stood facing her, his shoulders turned toward her, his head bent slightly forward, blinking his eyes rapidly and looking away a couple of times. Thomas had no trouble recognizing these instinctive codes of seduction that behaviorists have identified. Louise herself is not entirely indifferent to his efforts. She did that thing, brushing aside a lock of hair, which with her is a sign of tension.

They are dancing and Boris is holding her to him, caressingly. With every move, Louise's top rides up, baring her skin, and Boris puts his hand on her hip to turn her. Thomas discovers a feeling of almost physical jealousy that he did not know he had in him. When "Crocodile Rock" comes to an end and Boris suggests they continue dancing to a less feverish number, Thomas intervenes.

"Do you mind?" he says with a smile. "I'm just going to borrow my wife from you for one dance."

The tall blond man pretends to be amazed, but bows and kisses Louise's hand before moving to the bar. Louise's cheeks are pink from so much exertion. She relaxes indolently in his arms, rests her head on his shoulder.

"I never saw you as macho and possessive."

"I have to admit it was beginning to bug me watching him maul you. I'd also had enough of you wriggling about like that, in a state of excitement."

Louise steps back for a moment and gauges Thomas's expression. He was not joking.

"Excitement?" she protests. "And you say I was wriggling?"

"Yes. And I can also say you smell of alcohol, my love."

"You're not my father."

Louise stumbles, Thomas catches her and laughs.

"I'd just like to point out that you're drunk. And I will concede that the guy's not bad looking."

"Better than that. He's a really good dancer."

"Granted. Still, he was holding you a bit too close for my liking."

"Are you jealous?" She cocks her head.

"Yes, I'm jealous. Wasn't your husband ever?"

"Romain trusted me completely."

"It must just be me then, I know you can leave a man."

"I'm certainly not going to leave you for some Boris Fern."

"Oh? Is his name Fern?"

"If you put the TV on from time to time," she replies, "you'd know that. Everyone knows him. But I'm not the sort to fall in love with a TV announcer. I prefer psychologists who bet at the races. Are you picking a fight? Is that what's going on, you're picking a fight?"

"I'd never pick a fight with you. It would be stupid, and inappropriate. But when I'm jealous, I'll say so."

"I love you, you idiot," Louise whispers. "Anyway, you know that when I go out it's to show off my ass."

Thomas smiles, kisses the nape of her neck. In spite of everything, he doesn't actually mind if she shows it off, that ass of hers.

KARL AND LEA

. . .

KARL AND LEA HAVE PUT lots of gifts on the kitchen table. Forty of them because this morning Anna is forty years old. Gifts in every shape, every color, wrapped in crepe paper, in velvet, in tissue paper. A real surprise. Anna plays the part accordingly.

"Open them, mommy, open them," Karl and Lea cry while Stan cuts the little cake. She has already blown out the candles.

Anna opens them, alternating between large ones and tiny ones. In one, a stone painted bright red with a letter *A* in gold. In another, one of Lea's drawings, which Anna unfolds carefully. A ginger cookie that she eats immediately. A salmon pink hair band. A red rose that she quickly puts in a glass. A queen of hearts, drawn by Karl . . . Anna wants to open a small one with a star design, but Karl and Lea protest, insisting she save it for the very end. A small glass for drinking tea. A plastic knight, "to defend her," Lea explains . . .

One gift is different from all the others, smaller, more regular, more expensively wrapped too. She has seen it, she wants to put off the moment, but Stan nudges it toward her with one finger.

"Open it," he says. "Happy birthday, my darling."

Anna knows it is a piece of jewelry, probably a ring, probably gorgeous, probably priceless. She looks at her husband, shakes her head, her eyes shining.

"Thank you," Anna breathes. "You shouldn't have, Stan, you know very well why you shouldn't have. I can't accept it, you're setting a trap for me. You shouldn't do that."

"Shush. It's a ring, not a chain, not a padlock. I'm not buying you. You know that."

"I'll open your daddy's present later, kids."

Anna continues. So as not to disappoint Karl and Lea, she takes her time, but her high spirits have evaporated, every second suddenly weighs so heavily on her. Is this the last time they will celebrate her birthday as a family like this? In two months' time, Karl will be eight. Can she ask him to celebrate that birthday without his father, then without her? Anna's hands are shaking.

"The last present's the most important," the children cry. A scarlet envelope, inside, a sheet of white paper.

Lea has drawn a frieze around the margins, Karl has written on it in colored felt-tip pen.

The letter begins with "Lovely little mommy." It is the most banal children's letter, but every word cuts right through Anna. She reads it slowly, out loud at first, then quietly, ending in silence. When she has finished, she squeezes her children in her arms. There is a question in the letter. She replies with tears in her eyes: "Of course, my darlings, of course I'll never leave you. You're the loves of my life. The loves of my life."

THOMAS AND JUDITH

• • •

*T*HE WIND BLOWS through Louise's blond hair streaked with the white she now allows to grow in. It is a very mild winter day on the Normandy coast.

"Come and help us, mommy," says Maud, "Judith and me are going to dig a hole down to the water."

Thomas squints in the light. Louise is rolling on the sand with her daughters, all three of them wave. With every move Louise makes, Thomas feels a sense of wonder as he glimpses the cheeky little girl he never knew.

Judith runs over to him, she wants a waffle, she is the one who takes his hand and drags him over to the crepe stall. Because Thomas "saved her life," the child thinks, by some mischievous inversion of logic, that he is now her property. A waffle with sugar.

"Thomas?" Judith asks when Maud and Louise join them. "How did you meet mommy?"

She does not look away: she wants to know. Her cheek is white with sugar, Thomas wipes it with a napkin. Maud is also listening closely.

"I'll leave you to explain it," says Louise. "Make sure you tell it properly. I'll be right back. And can you order me a tea?"

Thomas tells them, in his own way. He tries to be accurate, talks about the first evening, the first exchange of e-mails, he even talks about the Galápagos iguana whose skeleton shrinks when there is not enough food. But Judith is not at all interested in the reptile.

"And did you fall in love with mommy right away?"

"I think I did," Thomas smiles, before correcting himself. "I'm sure I did."

"And did you know about daddy?"

"Yes," Thomas replies, as frankly as the question was asked.

Louise is back, she takes his hand.

"You know, my darlings," she says, "I've told you, there were already lots of things that weren't right between daddy and me. We used to be very happy and the proof is that you're both here, but we hadn't been happy for a few years, even if it didn't show. And then I met Thomas, and I really, really fell in love with him—in spite of his gray hair, I know—and everything felt so clear to me."

"What wasn't right, mommy?" Judith asks.

"For example, daddy and I didn't want to have any more children together. But I, well, I still wanted a baby."

"You want a baby, mommy?" Judith reiterated.

"Yes. Very much. Your daddy could still have one in five years, or ten years. But I'm a woman, it's not the same. I'm nearly forty, and if I don't have one soon, I won't be able to anymore, because I'd be too old, and that would make me so sad. Do you understand, girls?"

"Yes, mommy," Judith says, concentrating.

Maud nods her head. Louise drinks her cup of tea.

"Well, I think we've managed it, Thomas and me. And we're all going to have to move in together soon, into a bigger house. I'm pregnant. I've got a baby in my tummy."

Thomas looks at Louise, dumbstruck. She has not told him anything. She kisses him gently on the side of his head, takes Judith on her lap.

"I've known for exactly three minutes. When I went to the pharmacy, it was to buy a test."

"And does the test say if the baby's going to be a little brother or a little sister?" Maud asks.

"No, my darling, it just says that I'm pregnant. And I'm very happy. The baby will be here in seven and a half months."

"In September?" Thomas asks.

Louise nods.

"Hey, mommy?" Judith asks.

"Yes, sweetheart. I'm listening."

"Hey, can I have another waffle?"

ANNA

. . .

RAGONS AND WITCHES, shooting stars and planets spin across the white wall in Karl and Lea's bedroom. Lea chose this nightlight among all the others with their images of flowers and animals. Anna was not convinced, but Lea reminded her that dragons and witches do not exist, that no one should be afraid of them, and the argument was so rational it persuaded her mother.

"You have to go to sleep, children," Anna says.

But Karl and Lea are not tired. Lea jumps on her bed and asks for a story. Anna takes a big illustrated copy of *Alice in Wonderland* from the bookshelf. She reads for a few minutes. Lea falls asleep first, breathing peacefully. Anna continues a little longer for Karl. A big marmalade cat smiles in the middle of the page.

"Alice," Anna reads in a soft voice, "was a little startled by seeing the Cheshire Cat sitting on a bough of a tree a few yards off. . . . 'Would you tell me, please, which way I ought to go from here?' 'That depends a good deal on where you want to get to,' said the Cat. 'I don't much care where—' said Alice. 'Then it doesn't matter which way you go,' said the Cat."

Karl has gone to sleep. A blue witch on a broomstick launches across the door when Anna turns out the light.

Yes, Anna thinks, the Cat's right, when you don't know where you want to go, it doesn't matter which path you take.

ROMAIN

. . .

From: romain.vidal@parisdescartes.fr
To: danielreynolds@stanford.edu
Subject: associate professor

Prof. Daniel P. Reynolds
Leland Stanford Junior University
Dept of Evolutionary Biology

Dear Daniel,

I'm using this prompt means of communication because I'm delighted to confirm that I would very much like to accept the post of
Associate Professor for six months and to run the HumanL@nguage
project, as we discussed in Stockholm.

I will email you again shortly to let you know the dates for the
weeks when I will return to France, so that you can set up the
university schedule accordingly. I have arranged the details of

accommodation with John, and am planning to arrive next week to be ready for the first conferences.

I'm so happy that I'll be working with your team, with John and Marina.

With warmest wishes,
Romain Vidal

YVES AND ANNA

. . .

*Y*VES IS TRYING TO SPOT ANNA at the entrance to the Rennes Métro station. He cannot find her. She is just across the street, on the sidewalk. She cannot believe he has not seen her. It must be because he does not see as well as she would like to think.

They walk together until they come to a café, where they sit at a table outside. Yves does not like sitting outside, where Anna—on the grounds that they are exposed to prying eyes— is distant, untouchable. He is sure that, already, they both know there are things that have not been said. But before anything else, Anna tells him about yesterday evening, at a friend's apartment. She talks . . . about primitive communism, about a book that should be written on children's education, and Yves watches her more than he listens. He watches and wonders about his own feelings, his desire for her, about the gap between illusion and reality. He knows she is going to leave him, just when everything has become so clear to him.

Anna is talking about her husband, the things that connect her to him "incontrovertibly," that is the word she uses, and she comes out with: "Yves, I'll never be able to leave Yves."

The Freudian slip makes Yves smile, but he can tell that she will, she will be able to leave Yves.

He does not repeat the things that have been said a thousand times. Perhaps this time he would succeed in formulating them even better, but what would be the point? You cannot spend your days saying the same things around and around in circles.

In spite of everything, he does say: "You're leaving me because you've never known how to give us a future. That's the invisible barrier you've kept coming up against, like a moth against a windowpane. I should have guessed, the future wasn't for me: in your letters you always talked about might and could."

Anna says nothing.

"You were waiting for some sort of sign in the clouds," Yves goes on, "a bolt from the blue, what do I know? Some instruction from the world telling you you absolutely had to live with me. The sign never came, and it never will. It's not for the sky to send instructions. Nothing will come, and that's why I have to leave, it's as simple as that."

They stand up, he does not make a scene, he never has. The café where they are having lunch is called The Horizon. He merely points out the irony. And hands her an envelope.

"Here. I've written you a villanelle."

"A what?"

"A poem, a sort of round with the first and third lines repeated . . . You can read it later."

She puts the envelope in her handbag, carefully. Anna would so love it if, in just one letter, a man could change a woman's fate forever. Yves does not want to do anything to nurture that hope.

Even as they walk toward her car, when they really are going to leave each other, the happiness he feels from still being beside Anna is so strong that, right until the last minute, it protects him, stops him being entirely sad. A stroke of her hand, a kiss on her cheek, and her perfume, still. This will be his last sensual memory of Anna Stein. When he turns away from her, when he walks away, sadness will tear through him and a great void will open inside him.

Truman Capote could not finish *In Cold Blood* so long as Perry Smith and Dick Hickock had not been executed. He just cannot get any further with *Abkhazian Dominoes* so long as their relationship continues. This book which is about them will be written in the present tense. The present will definitely have been their tense. Of course the word also means gift. Let it be one.

He does not know this but behind him, Anna has turned around. She is watching him walk away. In a store window, just across the sidewalk, there is a pretty little dress, short, low cut, in blue cotton with drawstrings on the sleeves and a floaty flounced hem in navy tulle. Yves disappears at the end of the street, Anna has such a strong urge to cry, she goes into the store. She tries the dress on. It suits her so well.

THOMAS AND PIETTE

. . .

In the only photograph of Piette that Thomas still has, her lovely legs will be long and tanned forever. Thomas has burned all the other pictures he took of her, including the nudes she had such fun posing for. Before throwing each image on the fire, he described it quietly: "Piette sitting on a stone bench, naked, her feet on tiptoes, thighs spread, doing nothing to hide her pussy, elbows on knees, her head resting in her hands, staring at the lens and laughing," . . . or "Piette in the bathtub, with her chin on the white enamel rim, her buttocks emerging from the bubbles, as well as one foot."

The flames left nothing. This photograph that Thomas did not want to burn tries to comprise all the different Piettes. Lying on a bed in a white cotton dress, with her legs in the air, she is reading through the speech that a friend wrote for their engagement party. It was an engagement just for the fun of it, but Piette had thought big and invited fifty friends to her parents' old farmhouse.

Summer has started early, there is a warm breeze blowing and the sky is fittingly sky blue. They have put baskets of fruit out on the large table, apricots, cherries, the first peaches.

"Come with me," Piette says in Thomas's ear when coffee is being served.

In just a few days in Provence, her skin has caught the sun, her hair is lighter, and her nose and shoulders have a smattering of freckles. She is pregnant: beneath her dress her small breasts have grown heavier, become firmer, the nipples larger, and, as soon as they are alone, Thomas touches them gently, filled with emotion. Angels have pussies and breasts.

"Come," Piette says again.

She takes his hand, leads him down a path between the cypress trees. It takes them to a stream which has almost run dry, trickling over great slabs of limestone. They walk on and on through bottlebrush shrubs, stocks, and Jupiter's beard. Piette is the one who knows every plant by name. At a turn in the path, the brook flows into a Roman-style tiled basin.

"I always used to come here when I was little," says Piette. "I did watercolors. The only things I drew were caterpillars, centipedes, and scarab beetles, can you believe it?"

Yes, Thomas doesn't doubt it for a moment. There isn't a girl in the world more unusual than Piette. Later, he will take a picture of a stag beetle that she drew when she was thirteen, and have it framed.

"Do you think we'll be happy, Thomas? Tell me about our life, tell me."

Thomas tells her. The birth of Daniel (or Claire), the sleepless nights spent talking in the half-light, spent making love, the quarrels about whose turn it is to do the feeding, the first

steps, the first words, and getting old too, together, with no fears. He describes the buildings of steel and glass that the great architect Piette will design in London, Berlin, and Tokyo. "And Métro stations, Thomas," Piette says, "I want to build Métro stations." Fine, let's have some Métro stations.

Piette has lain down on the dried grass, she closes her eyes so she can concentrate on listening to Thomas, to his warm gentle voice rolling out the years to come. He says: "We'll travel, we'll take the children to the Greek islands." "Will you read them the *Odyssey*? Will you show them dolphins and flying fish? Will I teach Claire to swim in the Aegean?" Yes, that's right, Thomas answers every time.

Then Piette stands up, they walk around the pool and she puts her arms around him. The basin overflows through a small notch in the rim, they follow the stream through scrubland to a stone aqueduct like a miniature Pont du Gard.

The aqueduct spans a storm drain and carries the water to the large tank at Anselme de Montaîgu. The bridge is far too narrow to walk along, with a sheer drop of about twenty feet to the white rocks below.

Piette has stepped along the first few feet of the parapet.
Thomas stays behind, he reaches out to her but she is too far
away.

"Stop, Piette. It's dangerous."

She turns, standing on the stone bridge, her feet so close to the
void. She speaks softly and that very softness frightens Thomas.

"Do you think I'll be able to bring up our child, our children? I am ill, you know."

"I know, Piette."

Yes, Thomas knows. Manic-depressive psychosis, bipolar
disorder, hypomania, cyclothymia, he has learned all the words
along with Piette. He also knows every label on the boxes in
that little case that goes everywhere with her: lithium nitrate,
lamotrigine, benzodiazepine, and plenty more.

"Come back, Piette, please."

"What I've got is a piece of shit, Thomas, it's a piece of shit.
Somewhere in this jumble of me, there's a normal part, a part
that doesn't envy other people's ordered lives, but then it's my
bad luck that I also have the other part that does envy them.
Do you think I could ever be happier than I am today?"

"I promise you you can, my Piette. Come back."

"You're so soothing, Thomas, and I love you and my parents
love you too, they want you to save me because they've never
managed it. Why do I sometimes so want to be alive but also
already dead? Why?"

"I love you, Piette, you're scaring me."

"I don't want to die, I swear to you."

Piette grabs Thomas's hand, he draws her to him and holds
her tight in his arms, the precipice now far away. Tears stream
over their cheeks. She is still shaking.

"If this illness takes me away, Thomas, will you look after
the children?"

"Stop it, Piette. We'll come to see this aqueduct in fifty years' time, with the children, and our grandchildren."

"And our great-grandchildren too?"

Piette shivers, then falls silent. They walk toward the farmhouse, toward the party where people are already dancing. Thomas looks back at the stone aqueduct, the valley, and the olive trees in the sunlight, almost a Cézanne. It is the last time he sees it.

All his love will be unable to save his Piette or to triumph over her melancholia. In twenty-five years, Thomas's entire trajectory, all his knowledge and skill will strive to do only that, to save the life of a young dead girl. With analysis he has found his feet again, but accepted? Never.

Thomas puts the photo down on the desk. If Piette looked at him now, she would see a gentle smile on Thomas's lips. Something has changed, because he can now remember her and feel happy.

EPILOGUE

· · ·

TIME WILL HAVE PASSED. It will have worked its spell. A year, two years, perhaps more.

There will be a reception at the New Morning venue in Paris. Yves Janvier will have finished *Abkhazian Dominoes*, which will have a different name. He will have taken Anna's advice: love is in the title. This book, or another one, should mean—his new editor will tell him—that he now finds *his* readership. This party will celebrate its publication.

All the others will be there: in alphabetical order, because some sort of order is needed, Anna, Louise, Romain, Stan, Thomas. There will be a good reason for each of them to be there.

Anna's invitation will have arrived at rue Érasme a week earlier, on a Saturday morning. As Anna's name and address were printed, Stan will have opened the anonymous-looking envelope out of habit. Unsettled to see Yves Janvier's name, he will have pulled himself together before handing the invitation to his wife without betraying any feeling. She will put down her cup and he will watch as she in turn feigns the same indifference. He will be grateful to her for this tactful lie. Anna will simply say: "Yves Janvier? He's a friend. I'll go."

But speaking his name will make her shiver.

"I'll go with you," Stan will say provocatively. "We'll get someone to babysit."

Anna will add nothing to this. She will talk about something else. A minute later she will drop her cup.

Louise will go as Thomas's guest. He will have met Yves the previous year when, after a public reading, he will have asked him for a dedication. Hearing his name, the writer will look up, an ironic smile on his lips: "Aren't you the analyst of a friend of mine?"

"She has finished her analysis," will come Thomas's reply.

The two men will be friends from then on, good friends. But every time Yves talks about Anna and the regrets that refuse to die, Thomas will remain very discreet.

As for Romain, his presence is easily explained. He will have recently started overseeing a popular science collection for Yves's publishers. He will be surprised to see Louise at the party. He will be thinking about remarrying. The future Mrs. Vidal will be called Natalia Vassilievna and will be twenty-nine. Without even knowing her, Louise will find her annoying. The future will prove her partly right.

After the inevitable speeches, when a group of klezmer musicians, friends of Yves's, step onto the stage, Anna will make her excuses and slip away for a moment. When she is alone, she will search through her bag and open a very worn envelope. It holds a poem that she has read many times over.

I wanted to write a villanelle for you
To talk of fleeting time that leaves no trace,
For Anna who leaves like the morning dew

Pain and time are sometimes one, not two
And love itself has a fragile transient face,
I wanted to write a villanelle for you

What lies ahead in life, I have no clue
I must find within me the courage to embrace,
For Anna who leaves like the morning dew

Lightning bolts, fire and sparks I eschew
I need no shield to hide my face,
I wanted to write a villanelle for you

To life alone do we stay true
But desire should be given its rightful place,
For Anna who leaves like the morning dew

Rugged is our path, harsh through and through,
In the shadow of poets we venture and pace,
I wanted to write a villanelle for you,
For Anna who leaves like the morning dew

But that's enough about love.